THOMAS LOCKE is an exceptionally creative author with a love of adventure and mystery. For his work on THE SPECTRUM CHRONICLES, he has been honored as a finalist for the C. S. Lewis Award. In this last book of the series, Locke offers the young adult audience yet another thrill-packed tale with a spiritual message that spans both worlds.

"Written with amazing foresight and ingenuity, this book is great entertainment reading. Highly recommended for those who like science fiction and outer space."
   Librarian's World
   (praising *Path Finder*)

THE SPECTRUM CHRONICLES

4

HEART CHASER

THOMAS LOCKE

BETHANY HOUSE PUBLISHERS
MINNEAPOLIS, MINNESOTA 55438

Heart Chaser
Copyright © 1997
Thomas Locke

Cover illustration by Joe Nordstrom

Published by Bethany House Publishers
A Ministry of Bethany Fellowship, Inc.
11300 Hampshire Avenue South
Minneapolis, Minnesota 55438

Printed in the United States of America.

Library of Congress Cataloging-in-Pub on Data

Locke, Thomas.
    Heart chaser / Thomas Locke.
       p. cm. — (The spectrum chronicles ; #4)
    ISBN 1–55661–921–9
    [1. Science fiction. 2. Christian life—Fiction.] I. Title.
II. Series: Locke, Thomas. Spectrum chronicles ; 4.
PZ7.L79425He   1996
[Fic]—dc21   96–45837
                                                        CIP
                                                       AC

—One—

Eleven days had passed since their successful attack on the pirate stronghold. Eleven days of powering along the lightway course, headed for the Solarus system. Eleven days without another contact with pirates or a single message from Wander.

The silence took its toll on Consuela. She kept up steady watches, searching the darkness of space with her heightened sensibilities. Yet in truth the danger of pirates did not keep her in the control room as much as the hope of another word from Wander.

Sleep did not come easy to her during that eleven-day voyage. Her dreams were filled with images of Wander crying out to her, the message lost because she was not listening. She remained tired much of the time and gradually became more withdrawn.

On the last day before their arrival at Solarus, Consuela remained at her station for hours after her watch had ended. Captain Arnol had warned her that as Solarus contained a Hegemony military base, she would not be able to search far afield. There would be too great a danger of being detected. So she stayed and she searched until her weariness rose and fell like great waves and she stumbled out of the control room and fell into her bed.

The dream that came upon her then was so vivid that she felt as though she had returned home. And yet Consuela knew she was dreaming. She stayed locked in this in-between state until she was awoken by the chiming of her communicator.

She did not want to wake up. The dream was both powerful and radiant. But the chiming refused to go away, until she managed to rise and key the switch and hear the order for her to report immediately to the control room.

Consuela arrived just in time to hear Captain Arnol sternly announce, "It appears that we are faced with the unexpected."

Consuela fought to bring herself to full alert, but it was hard. She sat across from Pilot Dunlevy, the young man who had joined them on the planet Avanti and had worked with her through the recent attack on the pirate stronghold. Dunlevy's normally gentle manner mirrored that of Arnol's. The pilot station of their spaceship, under ordinary circumstances spaciously comfortable, was crowded with five chairs encircling the console. Guns and Rick sat on Dunlevy's other side, their gazes as focused as gun barrels.

"You're saying we've hit trouble," Guns, the senior weapons officer, said.

"Not yet," Arnol responded. "Not necessarily."

Consuela struggled to set aside the lingering remnants of her dream—or had it been a dream? She was not sure. She had seen little that she recognized, but the experience had been so vivid that she wondered if she had actually been back on Earth.

"It could be a routine garrison inspection," Dunlevy agreed. But his tone did not match his words.

Consuela swept sleep-tousled hair back from her face.

The summons had carried such an urgent note that she had leapt from her bunk, slipped on her robe, and rushed with him to the pilot station. But still her mind was caught in tendrils of the image she had left behind.

She glanced over at Rick, who responded with a grin. Her only companion from Earth was as reckless as he was handsome and possessed the courage required of a good combat pilot. That was the position he held now. Back home, he had been a local football star. She seldom thought of those things nowadays, what with everything that was pressing on her here. But the dream still lingered, and with it all the memories of Earth and her life before the sudden transition.

Guns leaned his elbows on the console and said, "Are you talking about Imperial troopers?"

"If it were only dragoons, we would have little cause for concern. Solarus is home to a substantial garrison, so we would expect to find them everywhere," Arnol replied. He turned to the ship's chief pilot named Dunlevy. Captain Arnol ordered, "Tell them."

"When we came out of n-space I made the standard check-in with the watch communicator at the Solarus main port," Dunlevy told them. It was he who had spurred Consuela to first search for Wander after he had been kidnapped by Hegemony dragoons, and then travel with Arnol and Dunlevy in their hunt for pirate strongholds. "Suddenly there was absolute panic in the tower. The communicator went berserk and started babbling like a novice scout. I was able to linger and listen in." His face looked as though it had aged ten years. "Two Imperial battleships appeared out of n-space directly above the port, with no notice whatsoever, and demanded immediate docking."

Guns looked from the pilot to the captain and back again. "Two battleships, and you say this is not trouble?"

"We do not yet know that our arrival and theirs are connected," Arnol reminded him.

"Captain!" the watch officer sang out. "We are now within range of their local communications."

"Request assignment of a parking orbit," Arnol ordered. And to the group, "We need time to plan."

A moment's delay, then, "Request denied, Skipper."

Arnol swiveled his chair fully about. "Remind Solarus port that Avenger is a ship designed for mining a gas giant, and that our dimensions will totally dwarf their port."

Their spaceship was indeed a mining vessel, one shaped like a top and as tall as the valley where it had been constructed was deep. But it was also a battleship, secretly designed and armed to fight the pirates that had been ravaging the planet of Avanti. Consuela was on board as a Sensitive, a pilot-in-training with remarkable abilities.

After another moment's delay, the watch officer reported, "Solarus port acknowledges message and says it is relaying orders for us to make for Docking Station Five."

"*Relaying orders*, is it," Guns muttered. "And with two Imperial battleships just landed?"

"Not good," Arnol agreed worriedly.

"Never heard the like," Guns went on, "not within the empire's center and this far from a trouble spot."

"No, nor I," Arnol agreed. He turned back and said to the officer, "Confirm receipt of orders. And thank them. Make it sound as though we are pleased with the *offer* of landing space. Request as swift a turnaround as possible. Inform Solarus we wish to off-load cargo and immediately make way for Yalla." He started to turn back, then checked himself. "And maintain constant watch over all comm-links. Let me know of any unusual traffic."

"Aye, Captain."

The sudden appearance of Imperial battleships brought

grim expressions to the faces of all gathered. In their successful attack on a pirate stronghold, they had found evidence which suggested the Imperium and their supposed pirate enemies were in fact allies.

The control room's main doors slid open, and the bearlike form of Chief Petty Officer Tucker appeared. "You sent for me, Skipper?"

"Yes. Come join us." Chairs were slid about, and Tucker eased his great bulk onto the station railing. He listened as the captain gave a swift overview of what had occurred, and his face grew graver by the second.

Consuela tried to concentrate, yet part of her mind still was held by the dream, if that was what it had been. She had found herself standing in front of an utterly unfamiliar church, the broad stairs rising to an entry ringed by great columns and crowned by a towering steeple. The doors had been closed, and somehow she had known that the church was locked shut. She had stood there, a soft wind blowing against her face, no one else around, and sensed that there was a message waiting for her. Something important.

Then Dunlevy had rung for her, and the urgency had pulled her away so swiftly that she felt as though she straddled two realms, the one of her dream and the one before her now. And the message still eluded her.

"I have to agree with Guns, much as it pains me to do so," Tucker said, when Arnol was finished with his recounting. "Two Imperial battleships arriving and demanding landing space is not the mark of an ordinary garrison inspection."

"I agree." Arnol reflected momentarily, then turned back to the officer manning the center console. "Do we have the in-system flight coordinates?"

"Just coming in now, Skipper."

"Let me have them."

There was a tense silence as Arnol reviewed the flight data. He looked up. "Petty Officer, you served time in the Solarus system, if I recall."

"Aye, Skipper." Tucker grimaced at the memory. "Duty officer on their rust bucket of a satellite refinery, promoted to master of the lunar landing station. Two of the longest years of my life."

"What do you recall of the inner moon?"

"That's where I was based." Tucker's broad features creased in a rueful grin. "Closest to a frontier port you'd ever care to find inside the Hegemony. Solarus mines turn out a high grade of iridium ore. There are also a few veins of gold, rich enough to send the rumors flying like sparks off a miner's drill. Strikers from all over the system make for here, hoping to open up the lost lode and make their fortune."

"A dangerous place, then."

"More like wide open, if you see what I mean, Skipper. Dangerous only to the unwary. A wild place, that moon. Handles a lot of secondary cargo traffic for ships not willing to pay Solarus landing fees. Lot of coming and going."

"That settles it, then." Arnol's tone took on the solid definition of command decision. "Guns, Tucker, I want you to ready your men."

"Sir?"

"Our approach takes us within close range of their moon. On our convergence, we're going to stray a bit closer still."

Guns and Tucker exchanged astonished looks. Guns said, "You're planning on off-loading us, Skipper?"

"We are supposed to be an unarmed mining vessel," Arnol replied, his tone crisp now that the decision had been made. "We have to be prepared for an Imperial inspection. That means most of our warriors and our weapons must immediately be made to disappear. Tuck, a vessel our size will look odd without a transporter of its own. So you'll take one and leave us the other. I want you to hand-pick your most seasoned troopers, Petty Officer. And fill the hold with weaponry. To the brim."

"Aye, Captain."

"Guns, you're going to have to disguise those attack pods. Will paint adhere to their surface?"

Their attack upon the pirate stronghold had been successful largely because of these fighter pods, or Blades, as they were known among the warriors. Constructed of the rare substance that was supposedly used only on Imperial battleships, the pods had cut through the pirate's defenses like a knife through butter. But to have the Blades discovered on a supposedly unarmed mining vessel would have meant the doom of everyone on board, and seal Avanti's fate.

"I can't say if it would work or not, Captain," Guns replied slowly. "I've never heard of anyone trying to paint elemental trinium before."

"Do what you can. It is essential that all prying eyes see nothing more than an in-system transporter with a contingent of simple guard pods." He inspected the two men, making sure they understood what he intended. "Just exactly what a mercenary outfit would possess."

Guns nodded slowly. "You want us to pretend that we are hiring ourselves out."

"Maybe to one of the outlying miner asteroids," Tucker offered.

"If worse comes to worse, yes." Arnol hesitated, then went on slowly, "We must prepare for the off chance that this is more than coincidence, gentlemen. I want you to see if there is an alternate means for your traveling on to Yalla."

Astonishment mounted to alarm. "Without you?"

It was vital that they journey as swiftly as possible to the Yalla planetary system. A second young trainee pilot named Wander, a young man with the most astonishing level of Talent discovered in recent years, had been kidnapped by the Imperium. He had managed one brief connection with Consuela, whom he deeply loved. In it, he had described the prison planet where he was being held. Yalla was as close a genuine destination as they could manage. It was of critical importance to Avanti's future that Wander be found and brought back safely. Only with his and Consuela's combined efforts could the pirates be kept at bay.

"You will proceed without us only if necessary," Arnol replied. "Still, it cannot hurt to prepare for the possibility. And see if an alternate means of getting our forces swiftly and secretly to Yalla might exist."

They mulled that over in silence, until Guns pointed at Consuela and asked, "What about the lass here?"

"A good thought," Arnol agreed. "She must go with you. Her presence on this journey is a secret. As you know, all records have her remaining as a guest of the Chancellor on Avanti. Try and keep it that way. And mind you keep your troopers on their best behavior."

"No worry about that, Skipper," Tucker agreed, with a wink for Consuela. "The lass here is their prize mascot."

"Brought us the first successful attack against the pirates ever, far as I know," Guns agreed. "She'll be handled like spun glass, or I'll be knowing the reason why."

"I seem to recollect seeing a portable pilot's training station among the stores to be transshipped on Solarus," Tucker added.

Consuela brightened at the news. A pilot's station was required to focus. Her special sentivities allowed her to communicate with other stations. Equipping the transporter with a portable station meant she would be of some real use during this expedition.

"Excellent," Arnol said. "You have my permission to appropriate it." His gaze shifted from Consuela to Dunlevy and back. "For reasons of security, you two will be our only link. Even so, you must hold yourselves to minimum contact. I shall expect you to do everything possible to elude any monitoring."

"Aye, Captain," Dunlevy responded for them both. "We'll make arrangements."

"Very well." He stood, drawing the others with him. "And be ready. There may very well be unwanted eyes watching us already."

Be ready. The words seemed to explode within Consuela's mind. *That* was the message she had been searching for within the dream. Again the image of the church with its closed doors loomed within her mind. But what did it mean?

"Watching only if they are really after us at all," Guns added.

"We must hope for the best and prepare for the worst," Arnol replied grimly and rose to his feet. "Ready yourselves and your equipment. On the bounce."

–Two–

Later, Consuela found Rick collapsed in a sweaty heap beside a pile of paint-covered rags, a steaming mug in one hand, a thick sandwich in the other. He scarcely had the strength to raise either arm. He watched her approach and said, "You almost look like one of us."

Consuela raised her arms to show off the one-piece suit of pearl gray mesh. "It's been so long since I've worn anything except scout robes that I feel a little, well, exposed."

Guns chose that moment to walk over and deflate onto the pile of rags beside Rick. "If I have to look one more minute at what they're doing to our babies I'm going to shoot somebody."

"I thought of that too," Rick said, "but I didn't have the strength left."

Consuela looked from one to the other. "What are you two talking about?"

Guns accepted Rick's offered mug, then cocked a thumb and said to Consuela, "Just have a gander around the corner there, if you've got a strong stomach."

Consuela walked over, peeked into the main hold, and gaped. "What in the world?"

"Paint wouldn't stick," Rick said tiredly. "We tried."

"Aye, they'll be scraping gray gunk off the gunnels for ages to come," Tucker agreed, walking over. The chief petty officer was coated in gray paint and sandy goo from head to toe. Even so, he managed a tired smile for Consuela. "Hello, lass. You look the proper spacer in that getup."

But Consuela could not take her eyes off the Blades, the attack pods they had to camouflage. "But they look *awful*."

Guns nodded once. "I think that about sums it up, don't you, lad?"

"Sounds right to me," Rick agreed.

Tucker explained, "A ship made of elemental trinium and not bearing Imperial Hegemony markers would raise the alarm from here to the Outer Rim."

"I know that." Consuela raised a protesting hand toward the Blades. "But that is—"

"A proper subterfuge," he finished. Though he shared their fatigue, Tucker was obviously pleased with his handiwork. "We mixed up a batch of the same plasteel we use for sealing holes and building temporary supports, see, and then we blew it hard and fast over the pods. The stuff dries in seconds, so even though it didn't stick to the surface, it formed a shell." He glanced at the nearest Blade and amended, "Of a sort."

"Sort of, is right," Consuela agreed. The sleek black one-man attack ships were gone. In their place were sickly gray blobs of what appeared to be dried mud. They cascaded in frozen glops toward the floor, forming teardrop shapes. "How do the pilots get in?"

"Oh, we drilled a hole down toward the base." Tucker could not completely hide his smile. " 'Course, some pilots have more trouble climbing aboard than others."

"I didn't see you offering to play the space monkey," Guns snapped.

"Ah, Guns, me lad," Tucker said, letting his chuckle loose. "I wish you could have seen yourself wiggling in that first time, truly I do."

Consuela pointed at the shape and demanded, "How do they *see*?"

"Ah, now, that's not a problem, I'm happy to say." Tucker turned back and gave the Blades a look of pure admiration. "They may be small, but those pups were built proper, I can tell you."

"Nice to see you finally admitting to that fact," Guns said.

"I've never had a problem with the Blades," Tucker said, not turning around. "Just with some of the flyers."

"When you put the shields on full, they stop everything." Rick spoke to Consuela from his bulkhead perch, ignoring the banter of his superiors. "I mean *everything*, including light from the visible spectrum. So when they designed the viewing system, they figured out some way to extend the 'eye' out beyond the shield. Don't ask me how, but they did. And the shields are farther out than that, that . . ."

"Disguise?" Tucker offered.

"Monstrosity," Guns responded.

A voice from the central lift-well chose that moment to snap out, "Ten-hut!"

Despite the fatigue, which had etched its way deeply into their features, Guns and Rick rose to their feet and stiffened as Captain Arnol strode into view. He glanced at their paint-spattered forms and said, "At ease. Do we have success?"

"Of a sort, Skipper," Guns replied glumly.

"Aye, sir," Tucker responded proudly. "Come have a look."

Arnol marched around the bulkhead, looked into the main hold, and winced. "Was that necessary?"

"Afraid so, Skipper," Guns said, his tone morose.

A flicker of mirth plucked at the edges of the captain's mouth. He struggled for a moment, then managed to bring it under control. "Well, there is one thing for certain. No one is going to mistake them for Blades."

"There are all sorts of craft used in-system where there are mining jockeys at work," Tucker agreed. He waved a hand at the lumpy vessels and explained, "A fellow trying to hunt for gold or iridium on a wish and a tight budget will buy whatever is cheap and works. Oftentimes this is nothing more than a chunk of asteroid. They'll hollow it out, fit it with a power plant, drive, and shields, and off they go."

"Then you gentlemen should fit right in." Another hint of a smile, then the captain's habitual grimness settled back into place. "I have some news."

"Can't be good," Guns said. "Not if it's brought you down here."

"It's not, I'm afraid." He turned to Tucker. "Have you selected your men?"

"Aye, Skipper. Everyone who's got full warrior status or seen enough battle duty so it would appear on their records. Nineteen in all."

"What about the pilot's console?"

"Just finishing with the hookup now, Skipper."

"And the weapons?"

"The transport holds are crammed tight," Tucker replied. "Everything else that would look odd on a vessel being transported across the Hegemony for delivery is netted and ready for jettison, if it comes to that."

"It already has," Arnol said crisply. "We have received another communication. We are ordered to prepare to receive an official delegation from Imperial Command as soon as we land."

The news settled over the group like a somber sheathe. Guns was the first to speak. "Any idea why?"

"None."

Guns nodded slowly. "We'll need to be pushing off, then."

"In a moment. Are the men gathered?"

"Ready and waiting, sir." Tucker amended, "Though a mite worse for wear, if you know what I mean."

"A weary and dirty appearance would not be bad in itself, for a team coming off mining work." Arnol nodded toward the main hold. "Call them to order, Petty Officer. I want to say a few words."

When the men were assembled, Arnol inspected them one at a time. He possessed the leader's rare quality of making each man in turn feel singled out. "By now, you have heard why this operation has been required," he began, his voice sharp and reaching to the farthest corner of the hold. "We have unwanted visitors approaching even as we speak. I do not know what this entails, nor what will happen once we make contact with the Hegemony commander. But this I do know. Whatever happens, the Avanti system is counting on us. Her people have invested years of work and a great deal of their dwindling wealth to get us this far."

He stopped there, allowing the echo of his words to ring through the great hold. Again there was the searching of each face in turn, then, "Guns, Tucker, stand forth."

Infected by the moment's solemnity, the two grizzled veterans marched forward two steps, turned smartly, and saluted with identical sharp motions. "Guns, I am placing you in command. Tucker, you are acting number two." Steel gray eyes bore into each man in turn. "I am also hereby ordering you both to set aside whatever contest there has been steaming between you, is that clear?"

There was a fair amount of coughing in the ranks as the

two veterans snapped off, "Aye, aye, Captain."

"I want you all to understand how serious this is. We have the hopes and needs of Avanti and her sister worlds riding with us. Make no mistake, we are their last chance. Even if the resources were available, they could never duplicate the secrecy that has surrounded this mission. The Imperium would be watching too closely."

He waited through another silence, then snapped out, "Guns!"

"Aye, Skipper."

"If for any reason we and the main vessel are diverted, I hereby order you to do whatever is necessary in order to successfully carry out your dual missions: Attack the pirates wherever you find them. Rescue the Talent Wander and return both him and Scout Consuela back to Avanti."

"But Skipper—"

Arnol leveled a gaze at Guns that would have melted steel. "Did you hear me?"

Guns snapped back to attention and cracked out, "Aye, Captain. Loud and clear."

"Very well." Arnol turned back to the team. "Whatever happens, whatever we face, you are hereby commanded to carry out your orders. And make heroes of us all."

– THREE –

The transport was a big bus with tiny side-windows and no wheels. Consuela kept telling herself that, and it helped. Otherwise she thought at times her heart would leap from her chest with excitement.

They had set up her console alongside the communication officer's station. The barrier separating the cockpit from the bus proper had been removed in order to make room for her. She sat directly behind the first officer, slightly raised as her chair was bolted to the console's portable amplifier, and it to the floor. The perch granted her an uninterrupted view through the front portals. The spectacle unfolding before her was truly awesome.

The first officer swiveled around and said, "Coming up to the first mark, Scout."

"Thank you." Consuela tore her eyes away from the rising vista and fitted on the dampened headset. She swivelled the miniature control-console toward her and ran through the conning sequence as Dunlevy had explained.

The portable console was, according to Dunlevy, a rudimentary affair, meant only to assist in training more scouts than could be accommodated at the pilot station. It was common enough in larger ships and active ports, as many pilots did not have the patience to stand full watches with trainees. They now intended to use it for communication between Dunlevy, who had remained back on the main vessel, and themselves.

Yet when she powered up, she grimaced as the squeal of an almost unbearble noise filled her head. She placed two fingers to each temple and leaned over, striving to concentrate enough to send the proper message.

"Is something the matter, Scout?" Tucker shifted his bulk about in the second officer's seat and gave her a look of concern.

Consuela raised one hand to silence him and sent out the words, *Scout checking in*.

Pilot here. Dunlevy's tone came back calm and reassuring. *How are you?*

Hurts. Consuela lowered the power gauge down to where the myriad of voices was reduced to a constant shrill static. *So many voices.*

Amp up, Scout. Can barely read you. As Dunlevy had suggested before departure, they refrained from using names. There was no way of telling who might be monitoring, or how closely.

Consuela increased the power and repeated her words. The background noise had the persistence of a dozen dentist drills working in her skull.

Her sensitivity was the only means by which they had tracked down the pirates, prepared for the incoming attack, and now were able to search for Wander. Yet at moments like these, when reaching out to communicate meant being battered by intense noise only she could hear, the strain was almost too much to bear.

Dunlevy thought a moment, then said, *I assume you can hear me all right.*

Consuela responded, *Affirmative.*

Then power up only to send. Dunlevy showed astounded humor behind his words. *Ask the flight lieutenant for his ETA.*

Consuela twisted down the power fully and looked up, only to realize that every eye in the transport was upon her. "The pilot asks when we are expected to arrive."

The first officer checked his chrono, and responded crisply, "One hour ten. Are you all right, Scout?"

"Yes, thank you." Consuela wiped at the sweat streaming down her face, then smiled as Tucker passed her a hand towel. She powered up and sent the time, then instantly cut back the comm strength.

The Imperial Hegemony has arrived in the form of a battalion commander, a senior pilot, and a fleet admiral, Dunlevy informed her. *Not to mention a contingent of twenty fully armed dragoons as escort. They insisted on a formal inspection of the entire ship.*

Despite the strain and discomfort, Consuela felt a shiver run through her. *They were searching for something.*

My thoughts exactly. They were most angry by the time the inspection was completed. And confused. Clearly they did not find what they had expected. They have been closeted with the captain ever since. Dunlevy's concern came through loud and clear. *I fear the worst. Best you inform the others. Check back this time tomorrow.*

And this noise?

You are picking up on Imperial traffic, Dunlevy replied. *Even I can catch segments of it now and then. This is good for us, as so much traffic will mask our own communications.*

Until tomorrow, then.

Consuela powered down, stripped off the headset, and leaned back against the seat. She felt exhausted.

"Here, Scout." A cool cup was pressed into her hand. Consuela looked up to see Tucker leaning over her. "Is there anything we can do?"

"I'm fine, really. It's just . . ." She struggled for a way to explain. "There's a lot of confusion."

Tucker kept grave eyes upon her. "From the console?"

She shook her head. "From the Imperial battleships."

The entire transport braced at her words. Consuela took a breath and explained what Dunlevy had reported. When she was finished, there was a long silence. Consuela was content to wait and sip at her cup. Then the communicator asked, "Should I relay this to the pods?"

"It can wait until we are safe on the ground." The first officer, though young, bore the same grim determination as Captain Arnol.

"Too much chance of being overheard, this close to a base," Tucker agreed.

Consuela took another sip and glanced through the front portals. She caught sight of a rock-shaped pod floating off to their left and wondered if it was Rick's. For a brief instant, she found herself envying Rick's easy way with these newfound friends. But she knew it was simply not her nature. She had always been reserved. The gift she had found waiting for her here in this realm, this extraordinary sensitivity, conformed to who she already had been on Earth. As though the gift melded to her reserve and granted it meaning.

She kept her gaze on the front portals. Despite her time in space, nothing had prepared her for this approach to a lunar landscape. The eerie vista drew her away from both her thoughts and her discomfort. She had never imagined that anything could look so utterly alien, so totally void of life.

The sky was made even blacker by the moon's silver-white scenery. Stars rimming the horizon grew ever more distant at their approach. The horizon itself was brutally jagged, as the moon's mountains had never known the wearing power of wind or rain. Even from this height, the peaks looked impossibly tall.

Directly beneath them spread out a great valley, the floor scarred with manmade domes and rutted tracks and circular meteor craters. Against the lunar backdrop, all man's efforts looked puny.

A sudden shaft of light pierced the blackness, forming a brilliant curtain toward which they floated. Consuela gasped and drew back involuntarily. Tucker grinned and said, "First lunar sunrise, lass?"

"First time on any moon, ever." There was none of the fresh wonder of an earthbound dawn. Instantly all was either burning brightness or impenetrable shadow.

"Just stay close," Tucker said, "you'll be fine."

"We're getting a signal from below," the comm officer said. "Wants our details."

"Here, let me handle that. Switch the signal to the overhead, will you?" Tucker accepted the hand mike, and when static hissed from the intercom, he said, "Come again, matey, we didn't catch you."

"Then open up your ears," snapped the speaker. "I don't like repeating myself, especially for rock hounds asleep at the wheel."

Tucker leaned back with a relieved sigh. "Happy, don't tell me they haven't given you a one-way ticket to the asteroids yet."

There was a moment's hesitation, then, "Tuck! You old scoundrel, is that you?"

"None other," Tucker replied jovially. "Good to know you're as full of smiles and laughter as ever."

"Full of spit, you mean. What brings you back to this forsaken hole?"

"I hear there's a mother lode just waiting to be dug out and delivered to market. Figure I and my men are the ones for the job."

There was a phlegm-filled laugh. "Then you're not the Tuck I know. He was always too smart to fall for that one."

Tucker shared an easy laugh, though it did not reach his eyes. "You've caught me out, mate. Truth be known, I got tired of the spit-and-polish routine. Put together a group of like-minded fellows, adventurers to a man."

"Mercenaries, you mean."

"I won't quibble with you, Happy. Know of any likely profits to be had?"

"Could be, could well be." The tone turned wheedling. "You'll remember your old mates if something comes up?"

"Always good to stay on your right side," Tucker replied. "You find us something, part of the proceeds will certainly find its way to your pocket."

"That's my Tuck," Happy said, suddenly eager. "You know where the north pit used to be? Sure you do, that was part of your old bailiwick. Been closed down, ran dry as a miner's graveyard close on five years back. It's our second landing field now."

"A second field," Tucker mused. "Things must be booming."

The old voice cackled. "You won't recognize the place, Tuck. See you when you've grounded."

Tucker spoke to the communications officer. "Make sure the off-riders caught all that."

"Off-riders, I like it." Guns' voice crackled over the intercom speaker. "You came through loud and clear, Tuck. We'll be following you in."

"Right you are." Tucker handed back the microphone,

and as he did the jollity slid from his features. He turned to face the silent transport. "You've all heard what we're up against here, and what our story is. Stick to it. Anybody asks where you're from or where you're headed, tell them to see me. Keep a sharp eye, a tight lip, and trust only your mates." He cast a solemn eye over the group, then added a final warning, "Folks in these parts have the habit of staying loyal only so long as nobody else offers them more."

–Four–

Wander stood alone in the floating station's corner as they descended into the great cavern. No matter how often he made this journey, he had never grown accustomed to the sight. The underground hall contained the mind generators, which used the planet's core as their energy source. Through these, Sensitives scanned the Imperium's vast reaches, a secret overview of the entire galactic regime. Wander stood by the railing, looking out to where the colossal chamber's edges were lost in haze and shadow.

As he stood, he paid careful attention to what was being said by the others going on watch with him. Wander had learned never to show how much he knew or what he found of interest. And their present discussion was fascinating indeed.

"They searched the mining ship Avenger from stem to stern," the senior monitor was saying. "And they did not find a thing. Nothing whatsoever out of the ordinary. It was just as the authorities back on Avanti had declared on the manifest—a brand-new gas planet mining vessel, outbound for Yalla."

Avenger was the name of Consuela's ship. Ever since the

day Wander had received Consuela's message of hope and promise, saying she was coming to rescue him from his fiery prison, the Hegemony-wide monitoring station on this planet called Citadel had known constant commotion. Watches had been doubled, with little reason given. Urgent and confusing orders had been received from Imperial Command, only to be countermanded hours later. The diplomat was seen raging in the halls, shouting at the guard sergeant responsible for the contingent of Imperial dragoons.

Rumors abounded. The Hegemony was being invaded by outworld forces. Pirates had been detected, proving the accusations of numerous planets. A strange new weapon had suddenly appeared out of nowhere, attacked an Imperial vessel, taken it prisoner, and vanished without a trace. Such hearsay flashed and sped through the stone corridors, only to wither and fade when no confirmation was received. In truth, the monitors knew nothing at all.

Wander had learned that the monitors longed after information from the outside. They remained bound to their work and their station, thrilled by the incredible power of Citadel's mind-amps. Yet they spent long hours of every watch in communication with Hegemony pilots, garnering every last shred of Imperial gossip.

The practice was officially frowned on, but in truth no notice was taken. To have restricted the custom would have resulted in a riot. Though only a handful of people, including the emperor himself, knew of the Citadel's existence, senior pilots were continually calling upon the monitors' services. Supposedly, the monitors were simply attached to Imperial Command, a vast space-bound organization that contained the emperor's official residence.

The monitors searched the far reaches of space, plotted unknown courses to newly discovered worlds, checked for dangers and possible attackers, watched over the turbulent outworlds. In return for their services, the monitors demanded nothing but a continual flow of news and gossip.

To have their news suddenly cut off, to be unable to determine what was happening, had every monitor on Citadel in absolute turmoil.

Digs sidled up to Wander. "Have you—"

Wander stopped him with an upraised hand. Although his talents had brought him to the attention of Citadel's three senior monitors, and his place was now much more secure, Digs remained his only friend. Digs understood the gesture. Realizing that Wander wanted to hear what was being said, he turned and faced out over the vast cavern beside his friend.

One of the monitors behind him demanded, "So they still do not know what it was that was behind the attack?"

"We still do not know," the senior monitor responsible for their watch replied, "if there has truly been an attack at all."

Wander kept his face turned resolutely toward the distance. The cavern's light was supplied by the transparent power line that ran through both the floor and the distant ceiling. They shimmered like brilliant veins. He struggled to keep his expression bland and listened intently.

"But the message from Imperial Command," another protested. "I heard it myself. They declared that an outstation had come under sudden attack, and that we were to monitor—"

"A message that was instantly countermanded," the senior monitor reminded him. "And a message for which there is now no record whatsoever. I know. I have checked. Twice."

There were three such floating stations interspersed throughout the great cavern. Yet since the disquiet began, all the monitors had begun gathering at the beginning and end of each watch to travel upon the central station with the senior monitor. This meant a very long walk for the lesser monitors and scouts such as Wander, as their stations were farther out toward the periphery, but he did not mind. It was vital that he hear and learn all he could. Especially when the talk was as today's.

"It is outrageous that we can be held to double watch-time with no explanation of what it is we are supposed to be searching out," complained another monitor.

"You are to search out anything unusual," the senior monitor answered. He attempted to be stern, but the fatigue in his voice drained his words of strength. "Anything at all."

"That is nonsense, and you know it as well as I," one of the monitors complained. "Forty thousand parsecs, two hundred and thirty systems, not to mention the outworlds, and nothing specific to guide our search. I have a good mind to complain to the diplomat."

"You would be well advised to stay as far from the diplomat as you possibly can," the senior monitor replied dryly.

There was a moment's silence, then a quieter voice asked, "Any word on what's causing the ruckus between the diplomat and the dragoons?"

The senior monitor sighed, and his answer carried a resigned weariness. "The dragoons are against leaving Citadel, and I must say with all this confusion I agree. But the diplomat has this girl, this young scout, so firmly fixed in his mind that he has overridden the guard sergeant's strongest protests. Protests which I must say I agree with, though you never heard those words from me. How a young, untrained scout stranded on Avanti could possibly be a threat to the Hegemony is beyond me."

Wander's grip on the railing tightened until his knuckles turned white. They were talking about Consuela.

"In any case," the senior monitor continued, "protest or no, the dragoons are ordered to Avanti. They are to ferret out this scout and bring her back here."

"And us?"

"We shall simply have to trust in our own monitoring skills, and in the Citadel's mystery." The station touched down with a gentle thud. "And now, to your stations."

Wander and Digs were starting down toward their secondary amp when the senior monitor called them back. He inspected them with tired eyes. "We are stretched to the limit. I hereby raise you to full watch status."

Digs and Wander exchanged startled glances, then chimed in together, "Thank you, Senior Monitor."

"Thank me when this is over. For the time being, you are assigned to, let me see . . ." He raised the keypad attached to his belt, read for a moment, then decided. "The seventh quadrant, yes, we've left that sector unattended for nine watches now. You understand the drill?"

"Report anything unusual," Digs repeated. "We understand."

He managed a weary smile. "It is admirable to see the eagerness of youth. This will look good on your records. Now to work, and good hunting."

As they hastened down the corridor between the two main amps, Digs hissed, "Freedom at last. You can't imagine—"

"I have to get a message to Avanti," Wander whispered.

Digs gave him a look of total alarm. "You can't be serious."

"I *have* to."

Digs slowed, stopped, inspected his friend. "It has something to do with our escape?"

The idea hit Wander with the strength of a thunderbolt. Instantly he knew the answer was a definite "Yes."

"Then I suppose we have to do it," Digs said, resigned. "But fast."

To either side of their passageway towered the great mind-amps. Their dark surface was translucent. Within their depths sparkled and flowed the power drawn from the planet's core. Usually Wander found their patterns mesmerizing. But not today.

"You two certainly took your time arriving!" The monitor stripped off his headset and pushed himself from the seat. "It is outrageous, scouts forcing a monitor coming off double-watch to hang about! The senior monitor will hear about this, mark my words!"

"It was the senior monitor who held us up," Digs replied, trying for quiet submission, but unable to keep his pride from getting in the way. "We've been assigned to stand full watch."

The monitor was so disconcerted he could not hold on to his anger. He glanced at Wander and protested, "But this scout's not been here long enough to learn his way around."

"I guess the senior monitor thinks we can handle it," Digs said loftily. He waited as the monitor gathered his things and left muttering. When they were alone, his nervousness returned. He whispered, "You really have to try this?"

"Right now," Wander replied firmly.

"All right, then, this is what we'll do." Digs bolted for the central station. "I'll power up the amp and take my own sweet time hooking in. I've got to do the paper work for the new shift, that sort of thing. You contact Avanti, then *immediately* head for the seventh quadrant, got it?"

"I won't stay an instant longer than necessary," Wander agreed, seating himself and fitting on the headset.

"If anyone catches wind of what you've done, we'll say you started off on your own and used Avanti to position yourself." Grimly Digs shook his head. "Which they'll believe for about a half a millisecond."

"Thank you," Wander said quietly, fitting on his headset. "Okay, I'm ready."

"Here goes, then." Digs hit the power switch, and as he receded into the temporal distance, hissed, "Remember, in and out *fast*."

With that first thrust of power, Wander speeded outward, coming faster into focus than ever before. His concentration was made diamond-sharp by urgent need. He rode the expanding force as if it were a great ocean wave, although it was normally not until the power expansion was completed that monitors began their own outward reach.

Avanti came into sharp focus. He followed the faint port signal straight down, tightened onto the tower, and signaled, *Urgent, Urgent, Avanti Port, Tower Control, come in.*

Immediately there was a response of total consternation. Then a shout of pain came across the way. *Watch Communicator here. Sorry. Spilled coffee in my lap. Who is this?*

Urgent, Urgent, Wander replied, almost shouting with the strain. *Have message for highest level. Can you record?*

There was a moment's delay, less than a few seconds, but long enough to make Wander want to scream with frustration and fear. Finally, *Ready to receive. Repeat, who is this?*

Friend of Avanti, Wander replied.

The reply became frantically excited. *Is this the Scout—*

Hold queries. Urgent, Urgent. Imperial dragoons are being sent to capture the Scout Consuela. Cannot give arrival time, but know they will be underway soon. Do you copy?

Copy. Finally, finally, the reaction was what he had

hoped for, crisp and sharp. *How large an invasion?*

Can't say, but rumor is it will be guards from Citadel only. Could be reinforcements from Hegemony, but there is much confusion, so perhaps not. Do you copy?

Message received. We will be ready. Many thanks.

Wait. Message continues. Repeat, these are Citadel guards. It would make my rescue much easier if you can hold the attacking force there. Copy?

We will do our best to tie them up in knots, came the delighted reply. *Glad to be of service to Avenger. Speaking of the ship, we have—*

Not now. Must depart. Message ends. Instantly Wander retreated and circled and powered out. He sensed Digs moving in alongside, and began reaching toward the seventh quadrant. Listening, searching as he did so, detecting no signal of his move having been monitored. Only when he arrived and began the normal routine did Wander take what felt like his first breath in hours, and feel the release of the steel band of fear that had been wrapped about his chest.

–FIVE–

Consuela watched through the front portal as two figures in spacesuits moved toward the transport. Together they dragged a chest-high accordianlike hose over and fastened it onto their airlock. As soon as the seals were in place and the double doors opened, a bandy-legged stranger pulled himself through and exclaimed, "Tuck, you old scoundrel! If you aren't a sight for sore eyes, I don't know what is."

"Likewise, Happy." At the back of the transport, Tucker straightened from his task of sorting. There was a narrow open space where the seats ended and a wall sectioned off a small 'fresher and a cabin with a half-dozen bunks. The space was now littered with weapons from the Avenger's aft hold. Tucker's bulk crowded the area as he waved the port official toward him. "Come have a seat. How you been keeping?"

"Can't complain, though I do anyway and all the time." The man was stubby in every respect—short legs, short jerky motions, a jutting chin upon a head that barely came to Consuela's shoulder. He wore a well-patched suit with port emblems so worn that she could make little out. His face was as seamed as a freshly plowed field, with all the furrows pointed downward, and he had the sourest expression she had ever seen. He made his way down the transport's crowded aisle with the ease of one long accustomed to the moon's lower gravity field, taking the stretch in easy leaps. He clasped Tuck's hand in a fierce grip and declared, "Whatever the ill wind was that brought you here, you'll live to regret it."

"Profit, just like I said," Tucker said briefly, and gave the trooper beside him a single nod. "Looks like everything's shipshape. You can repack."

"Right you are, Tucker."

Happy cast a shrewd gaze over the warrior's rigid stance and said, "Got yourself a packet full of ex-dragoons?"

"Not on your scrawny neck," Tucker replied, lifting one of the portable blasters and running his hand idly down the barrel. "But all have seen off-world duty of sorts."

"Planetary soldiers who wanted to see a bit more of the realm," Happy interpreted. "I like it. Seasoned soldiers are hard to come by for guard duty." He ran his gaze over the mass of weaponry set carefully out for his inspection. "Looks like you made off with the better part of somebody's arsenal."

"Picked up a bit of this and that, you know how it is," Tuck replied easily. "What was this you said about guard duty?"

Happy caught the interest and turned cool. "Oh, nothing much. Couple of caravans making for border worlds."

Tucker's tone matched Happy's pretended nonchalance. "What would a bunch of second-rate ore vessels need with guards, especially if they're staying within Hegemony boundaries?"

Happy tossed him an ancient gaze. "Where you been hiding, Tucker?"

"Here and there. Why do you ask?"

"There's changes on the wind, matey. None of them good. Solarus garrison is growing all the time. You know as well as I how cargo convoys would just as soon stay out of the way of dragoons and their commissars. Whatever is bought by the Imperium these days is paid for in Hegemony scrip, which is fine if all you're wanting is wallpaper. A lot of the upper-grade caravans have been forced to use us for their staging point."

"So that's why you needed the second landing station," Tucker mused. "Been wondering about that."

"Second and third and before too much longer, a fourth in the planning stages as well."

Tucker stretched his bulk in an easy yawn and said, "Caught some traffic about Hegemony vessels landing down on Solarus as we were pulling in."

"Don't know anything about that, and don't want to." Yellowed eyes turned shrewd. "You and the boys on the run?"

"Clean slates, the lot of us," Tucker replied, holding to the easy tone. "One of the requirements for signing on."

"Well, if that's the case, then you'll be having caravans crawling over each other to hire you on as guards."

Tucker turned to the listening crew and said, "That's the sound of profit if ever I heard it."

"You'll be remembering your mateys when it comes time to seal the bargain," Happy cautioned.

"If pickings are as good as you say," Tucker replied, "we'll be heading back this way again. We'll need to keep you on as permanent eyes and ears."

Happy showed as close to a pleased expression as he could manage, then leaned forward and said conspiratorially, "Something's got their wind up."

"Who?"

"The dragoons, the dark couriers, all the Hegemony parasites."

Tucker could not fully mask his surprise. "Dark couriers? Here?"

"On Solarus, or at least so go the rumors." Happy pretended to spit in disgust. "Rumors, you wouldn't believe how they're spreading. Word is, something's hit the Imperium and hit them hard. They're swarming about like crazy. Got everybody worried, especially the outbound caravans. You'll be in prime demand, especially if you can be ready to depart soon."

"Got nothing to keep us here, if the price is right."

"I'll see to that," Happy assured him.

"Of course you will," Tucker said. "Oh, by the way, as you were speaking of borderlands, keep your ears open. We've heard rumors of rich pickings out around Vector Nine. Any caravan headed toward that quadrant would be our first choice."

"Can't hurt to check," Happy said doubtfully.

Suddenly a voice came crackling over the intercom, "You plan on jawing all through the lunar day?"

"Guns," Tucker explained to Happy's startled expression. "Our number one outrider."

Happy squinted through the front window, then widened his eyes. "Those ugly suckers are guard pods?"

"I'm liking this man less and less," Guns said sourly over the intercom.

Happy shook his head in amazement. "I thought you mateys were towing some likely looking rocks, wanted to play at ore-hounds in your spare time."

"Why don't you string out a passageway," Guns barked, "so I can tell you personally what I think of your jokes."

"If they caught you unawares," Tucker said, "think of what they'll do to any incoming attackers."

Happy glanced back at the massed weaponry. "They well armed?"

"To the teeth," Guns snapped over the intercom. "Now hows about letting my boys and I out for a stretch?"

Happy turned back to Tucker and displayed the worst set of teeth Consuela had ever seen. "You're right, matey. There's the smell of profit in the air."

"Vector Nine," Tucker repeated, his tone as easy as his heavy-lidded eyes. "And a planet out there called Yalla. That was the world on everybody's lips. Just something for you to keep in mind."

–SIX–

Rick crawled from the claustrophobic tunnel, rose to his feet, and gave an enormous sigh of relief. It had felt more than strange, creeping along the flexible tube, nothing but the thin walls between him and utter vacuum. The tunnel was so narrow it had squeezed him from every side. The low gravity had not helped, for each scramble had pushed him up against the top, making handholds hard to keep and leaving his reflexes feeling out of sync.

"Rick." Consuela moved over in little airy steps, hands searching for the overhead holds. She stopped in front of him and began bouncing up and down, quick thrusts of her toes enough to send her several inches into the air. Her brown hair was caught back in a dark ponytail, which rose and fell in slow motion. "Can you believe this?"

He was about to say how good it was to see her smile, when a hand clasped his shoulder and Guns said, "That tunnel was something to remember."

"I felt like I couldn't breathe," Rick agreed.

"These middling trade moons are all alike, skimping on the basics." Tucker moved forward and stopped before them. "The upside is, the only way to the pods is first through the big passage here and then our transport."

"All it would take is one person in the know to clamber through the plasteel shell, look up, and see what the pod's belly is made of," Guns agreed. He glanced back at the small tunnel's branching and shuddered. "Though I can't say I'm looking forward to the return journey."

Tucker asked, "Ready to set up watches?"

Guns looked up at the burly man. "I'd say you can handle that as well as I."

"Arnol put you in charge."

"Aye, but the skipper's a good ways off just now." Guns kept a steady gaze. "My suggestion is we hold to equal status for the time being. Especially here, where you know the lay of the land. Then, if there's trouble, we go with the captain's orders."

Tucker held the wiry weapons officer's gaze for a long moment. "Nary another man I'd have to guard my back in a battle, Guns."

"Likewise."

Tucker turned to the transport, cramped now with the Blade flyers perched alongside the troopers. "Three watch shifts. We're all weary from the preparations and the journey. Still, we need volunteers for first watch. Whoever stays will have to keep on their toes. Nobody but nobody gets through the transport to the pods."

Consuela raised a small hand. "I just sat around before we left. The others should get a rest."

To Rick's surprise, Tucker did not turn her down. "It may be best for you to hold back until we've got the lay of the land. Mining towns can be rough places. Plus you'd be earning our thanks." He raised his voice. "Six more. No flyers, you boys have already done double duty. Who else?"

Rick stood isolated by his fatigue and the disappointment of not being able to stay with Consuela. He started when she touched his shoulder, leaned forward, and said quietly, "I went back to Earth again."

"What?"

"At least I think I did. It was a dream. But it seemed vivid enough, just the same." Swiftly she described the red-brick church with its great pillars and tall steeple. "Does that sound familiar?"

"Not that I can recall."

"Then I don't understand it." She seemed genuinely disturbed.

Tucker's voice brought them both around. "All right, those not assigned first watch, let's be moving out. Draw hand blasters from stores, but keep them strapped down; they're for show and not for use. Stay close, watch your mates, keep a sharp eye for trouble."

"Perhaps we can find a quiet moment later," Consuela said.

Rick nodded, grabbed his small pack, and allowed the crush to push him toward the transport's main exit. As he passed through the portal, he turned back, caught sight of Consuela's face, and saw her mouth the word "friends."

–SEVEN–

Rick stepped through the moonbase's massive airlock, looked around, and declared, "Party time at the OK Corral."

"I don't understand what you said, lad," Tucker responded. "But I agree with the sentiment."

The airlock door was as large as a bank vault. They gathered to one side in order to gain their bearings and allow the crush to pass them by. Rick glanced up, astonished at the cavern's size.

The only way to grasp its dimensions was to count the levels ringing the central open space, which itself was the length of five football fields. Rick started at the distant floor and counted up, was around halfway and at the number twenty-three when his sleeve was pulled and a voice said, "Got a berth, mate?"

Rick found himself staring down at an undersized man of leathery skin and ancient eyes. "What?"

"Frankie's is the place. Guaranteed clean, airtight, and secure as—"

"We're fresh caught, but not first-timers," Tucker rumbled easily, stepping forth. Then to Rick, "Check and make sure your pouch is still intact, lad."

"Hey, what kind of . . ." The man's backward progress was halted by Guns sidling up behind him. The voice became more plaintive. "This is a legit hustle, mateys."

Tucker's eyes remained on Rick. "Lad?"

"Everything seems intact."

"Best sling it under your poncho until you're used to the ways around here." Tucker's stubby fingers dug out a coin. He held it up so that it caught the light. "Dusty still running his hall?"

"You been gone awhile," the weasel replied, his eyes held by the coin. "Dusty don't do much but sit by the fire and spin his tales. His daughter's handling the trade. Good lass, name of Stella. Take you there, if you like."

"I know the way." Tucker flipped him the coin. "For your troubles."

They started off, Tucker at point and Guns holding the rear. All the group were tense, all eyes nervously scouting every shadow. Rick had trouble holding to the brisk pace. The moon's low gravity made walking a genuine effort. Plus he was as tired as he had ever been in his life.

Guns noticed his discomfort and moved forward to ask, "Your first time at low-g, lad?"

"Yes." Rick stumbled and kept himself upright by grabbing hold of Guns' shoulder. "This is a lot harder than it looks."

"Don't think of it as natural walking, that will help. Push yourself forward, then hold and wait for the ground to reach you." Guns repeated the instructions slowly, pacing him through the gait. "You're doing fine. Not long now."

Their walk took them along the same level as the airlock, perhaps a third of the way up the cavern. Below was a full-scale market, selling everything from foodstuffs to mining equipment. There were drills three times the height of a man and ending in an stubby black muzzle; Rick did not need to ask how he knew it was a drill and not some giant weapon. The flow of information remained available whenever he required something. It had been the same since their coming. Both Rick and Consuela had arrived with knowledge and talents intact.

Rick flinched as they passed a great doorway. The noise from within the bar's shady depths was deafening. Once past, he slipped up to Tucker and asked, "Was that music?"

"Of course." Tucker showed mock surprise. "It wasn't to your liking?"

"It sounded like a dozen chain saws chewing on nails."

"That was fairly tame for these parts," Tucker replied.

"Whatever you do," Guns added, moving up from behind them, "don't enter any such place alone."

Tucker directed them down a tunnel, five times Rick's height and as crowded as everywhere else. Men and women pushed along, the crowds thick and boisterous. Clothing was beyond weird—animal skins and chains and heavy boots, or shiny robes that billowed with each step, or tattered space suits minus helmets, or ancient uniforms with faded medals—a hodgepodge of colors and forms. The noise was continual and overloud, battering at him.

As though a switch were abruptly thrown, a wave of stillness passed through the throng. With the suddenness of an involuntary shudder, people pressed themselves up tight against the walls. Rick felt arms grasp his shoulders and ease him back, just as a figure came into view. It was an old woman, dressed in a robe so black it drank in the light. She was followed by men obviously matched for size and girth, so large she scarcely came up to their waists. The men wore golden uniforms that shimmered like a liquid field with each step.

"A dark courier," murmured the trooper next to him.

"What is a—"

Guns hissed a command for silence. The woman's gaze flitted over them. Rick felt the air freeze in his chest. He had never seen a gaze so cold. The soldiers wore gold helmets with blaster shields pulled down over their eyes. Their massive weapons were carried at parade rest, across their chests, and their gaze was constantly on the move.

Only when the woman and her entourage passed did the tunnel gradually come back to life. "Okay, let's move on," Tucker said, his voice subdued. "Not far now."

Rick moved back to where Guns watched their rear, and asked quietly, "What was that?"

"Dark courier," he said, his voice crisp with unease. "What the common folk call a senior diplomat."

"But who—"

"The Emperor's hounds. Wherever they go, doom and destruction soon follow." Guns cast an anxious glance behind them. "I'll be glad when we've left this system behind us."

"Those soldiers were something."

"Aye, Hegemony dragoons. Bloodthirsty lot. Imperial household guards, from the look of their uniforms. Though what the emperor's chosen few are doing on a minor outpost like this one is beyond me."

Rick recalled the moment that old crone's gaze passed over him, and shuddered. "That woman shook me up."

"Aye, anyone who says they're not frightened by a dark courier is a liar and a fool to boot." Guns pointed ahead to where a grim-faced Tucker was motioning them through a narrow portal. "Looks like we've arrived. Don't know what I want most just now, a meal or a bed or a ticket out."

Rick awoke to the sound of low voices. He rolled over,

and it was only his swift reflexes that kept him from falling from the narrow bunk. He unfastened the curtain, opened it a crack, and blinked at the bright light. When his eyes adjusted he saw that the central table of their chamber was now occupied by Tucker, Guns, and two strangers. A pair of guards—not theirs—stood at alert by the portal.

He slipped into his clothes, pushed the curtain wide, and dropped down. He slid his feet into his shoes, made his way to the 'fresher, and upon his return spotted a side table heavily laden with breakfast.

They had paid extra to have a private rock-walled chamber all to themselves. The chamber's only color was from the curtains shielding the floor-to-ceiling alcoves that lined three walls. Rick heard gentle snores coming from those nearby. He filled his plate, then turned to find Guns waving him over.

"This is one of our pod flyers," Guns said proudly, making room for him on the bench. "Rick, Mahmut here runs a caravan headed for Yalla."

"The desert planet is known for the beauty of its gems," the merchant offered, his voice as oily as his dark hair. His eyes were as black as onyx and as unreadable as the night. Mahmut offered Rick a smile that meant nothing at all and said, "Firestones are coveted throughout the Hegemony, even adorning the emperor's crown. Alas, the merchants of Yalla are well aware of the jewels' value, and charge us the moon and stars and sun and wind. It is very difficult for an honest merchant to make an honest living, much less pay the exorbitant amount requested by guard-captains."

Rick saved himself from needing to respond by keeping his mouth full. Tucker fired back, "We have requested a fair wage and not a penny more. Even the landing station's supervisor, the one all know as Happy, has said our price is low."

"And *I* say there is no need for further guards at all." The young cohort shared the merchant's slender build and dark complexion. His eyes blazed as he challenged each man in turn. "We are armed, our guards are well trained, and what's more, their trust has been earned over years."

"You must forgive my son," Mahmut purred. "He does not share my anxiety rising from this spate of rumors."

"There are always rumors in third-rate hovels like this," the young man said, his voice almost a snarl. "If we take them on, we'll have to assign our own guards to guard *them*."

"True, true," Mahmut grumbled, stroking his thin beard. He wore a gray belted robe over a singlet of black silk, simple yet clearly of finest quality. His single ornament was a ring with a stone the size of Rick's thumbnail, a jewel that seemed to flicker with a light from within. "It is indeed a dilemma. Perhaps if the guard-captains were to lower their price a trifle . . ."

"The price is fair and firm," Tucker replied tightly. "As to whether or not we are trustworthy, there are a dozen people and more around these parts who will tell you who I am."

"And profess to your honesty, yes, Happy has already brought several of these people for us to speak with. A most impressive show." Dark eyes flitted swiftly about, making it hard to get a fix on what the man was thinking. "Yet I am also wondering what argument you can make to my son's concerns."

"We won't argue with anyone," Guns replied. "But we also don't need access to your caravan or your goods."

The young man snorted. "That goes without saying."

"Abdul, please," the father murmured. "It is a fair offer. Hear them out."

"We are being hired as outriders," Guns persisted. "Your

first line of defense in case of attack."

"Not to mention my trained soldiers there to help your men stand guard wherever you ground," Tucker added.

"The planets we shall visit before and after Yalla are indeed lawless lands," Mahmut agreed.

His son objected, "And what if the pirates are using them as a first line of attack?"

"Pirates?" Rick pushed his plate to one side. "You've heard something about pirates?"

"Ah," Mahmut said. "The young flyer's interest is piqued at last."

"And not just his," Guns said. "We'd give our eyeteeth for another go at pirates."

It was Mahmut's turn to show a keener gaze. "*Another go?*"

"We're not sure what it was," Tucker said, shooting Guns a warning glance. "But we know something's out there, and we've tangled with them before."

"And not just you," Mahmut confessed. "Several of our merchant friends and their caravans have vanished without a trace. And, as I said, rumors abound." He glanced at his son. "Especially now. Especially here."

Sensing the argument going against him, Abdul chose another course. "I have seen these guard pods of yours," he snorted. "What makes them so special? It is certainly not their looks."

"A solid weapons system," Rick replied. "And training."

"Not to mention finely honed reflexes," Guns added.

Abdul's eyes glittered like a big cat hunting prey. "Ah, reflexes. How very interesting. They have a sport here that requires good reflexes. They call it ground-flying. Perhaps your pod flyer would be willing to have these reflexes of his put to the test."

Tucker's brow scrunched together in unexpected worry.

"I know this diversion. It's a suicide sport."

"The lad has never been on a low-gravity planet before," Guns added, "much less here."

"Our last journey was my own first visit," Abdul swiftly countered. "It was only then that I learned the sport myself. As to suicide, I have no intention of departing an instant earlier than necessary."

"Several of our guards have become passionate about this little game," Mahmut added, a flicker of humor deep within his gaze. "I assure you, gentlemen, I would not risk my valuable defenders at such an unstable time. The game has risks, yes. But so does life itself."

"And what better way to test these so-called reflexes," Abdul sneered, "than with a game he does not know?"

"I still would advise against this, lad," Tucker warned.

"Ah, of course, if your gallant flyers are afraid to have their courage tested as well," Abdul taunted, "we of course understand."

Rick met the son's flat gaze and replied calmly, "I have no problem with a contest."

"A wager," Mahmut cried. "Your young flyer will accept the challenge. If he succeeds, I agree to your price and terms. If not, you agree to mine."

"If not," Abdul corrected angrily, "we do not use them at all."

Mahmut hesitated, then waved his hand in agreement. "So be it."

"So the game is to beat you, is that it?" Rick watched the son and decided it would be a pleasure.

Abdul barked a laugh, his face taut with eagerness. "The game, fly-boy, is to survive."

–Eight–

"I still don't like it, lad," Tucker repeated for the dozenth time. He was cramped into the narrow seat beside Rick, his broad features furrowed with concern. Their transport was little more than an oversized pod, and jammed to the gills with people. "There're risks here you can't imagine. And the only one with you wants to see you lose."

"Too late to turn back," Rick said, glad his nerves did not show in his voice. "Guns and you have both been checking, and there aren't any other caravans headed anywhere near Yalla. We're committed."

"Aye, I suppose so." Tucker sighed past his objections. "All right, then, here's what I know of the contest."

Rick was overtall for the transport, and his knees were jammed hard into the seat in front of them. He glanced down at the helmet in his lap. Like the others around him, he wore a space suit as tight fitting and supple as a downhill skier's. Yet where his was a uniform gray, the others crowding the pod wore suits decorated with wild designs—racing stripes, angry masks, ferocious beasts, serpents weaving up and around their entire bodies. "Who am I up against?"

"This is not a contest against others," Tucker replied. "Against yourself."

There was no worry of their being overheard. The noise Rick thought of as chain-saw music raged from the overhead speakers. The shouted conversation among the other passengers was almost as loud. Tucker went on, "I had several mates who became hooked on ground-flying. It was a thrill like no other, they said. And the only way to survive was to be fully committed."

"Survive?" Rick examined the older man's somber features. "They used that word?"

"*Commit*. That is the word you need to concentrate upon." Tucker's expression was as fierce as Rick had ever seen it. "There is no safety in seeking control through slowing or stopping. The way makes any such movement unstable. You must *commit*, and stay committed to the end."

A slender figure, dressed in a suit of silver with purple lance-heads crossed upon the chest, bent over them. It was Abdul; he sneered at the pair and shouted, "Trying to give your mate a final lesson in courage?"

Before Rick could respond, wild cheers and shouts and war whoops rose until the music was drowned out. When they died down, Abdul shouted, "Too late for that! We have arrived!"

Rick let Tucker fit his helmet into place, waited until Tucker had adjusted his own, then joined the crush moving toward the portal. The din in his ears was overwhelming. Once outside, the view was so sudden and so shocking that Rick stood numb, immobile, until Tucker gripped his arm and drew him to one side of the platform away from the others. Instantly the din diminished. "Can you hear me?"

"Yes." But it was hard to concentrate on Tucker's words. "This is *awesome*."

But Tucker was too worried to pay Rick's excitement

any mind. "The radios have a range of only a few feet. The authorities insisted on it, as noise from the ground-flyers was interfering with work. The flyers accepted it as part of the game." He sounded disgusted by the idea. "Which means you will be utterly on your own once you start. Do you understand?"

"Yes." Rick did a slow pirouette. The pod had landed upon the highest peak in the lunar range. The crest had been leveled into a broad platform. As far as Rick could see in every direction was sky of jet-black, with millions of stars flowing like great silver rivers. And directly overhead hung Solarus, so close he could actually see the globe's curvature, a vast sphere of cloud-covered blues and greens. Beyond and to his right hung a second moon, a bright silver orb too brilliant to be so still.

"Ah, there you are." Abdul sauntered up, his derision coming loud and clear over the radio. "Sorry, nothing gained by hanging back, there's only one way off." His steps were turned into a mincing dance by the low gravity, his head a silver globe set upon the gleaming silver suit. He stopped a halfpace from Rick and added, "That is, unless you would like to withdraw now, and let us be done with you."

"I'm ready," Rick replied. This sort of banter was nothing new. Taunts like these were part of every line of scrimmage of every football game he had ever played.

"That's what you think." Abdul held out what at first glance appeared to be a broad plank. It was half Rick's height, with curved edges and a slightly uplifted nose. "This is your flyer. And your last chance to withdraw."

"I'll take that," Tucker said. He bent the board over his broad knee and began checking the edges and the foot straps. Finally he straightened and said, "It all appears to be in order."

"Of course it does. I do not need to resort to subterfuge," Abdul announced. "The course will see to that for me. That is, unless you—"

"Let me have a look at that," Rick said, reaching for the board.

"See you on the crown. That is, if you make it down at all," Abdul taunted. "Fly-boy."

"The crown," Tucker said, once Abdul had moved away. "Now I remember. They used to talk about that. The course enters a long straightaway—there are several, but this is longer and straighter than all the others combined. They call that the safety stretch. The flyer has two choices. Most do slow sweeping turns down the straightaway, bleeding off their speed. And remember, until you reach that last stretch you will need all your speed to survive. So make sure it's the last stretch before you start slowing down."

Tucker breathed heavily, worried beyond words by what was about to take place. He collected himself and went on, "At the end of that final stretch there is a broad overhang. Use the last of your speed to swing up the side and over the top. The pod will collect you there."

Rick kept his eyes upon the board in his hand and had difficulty not to laugh out loud. "And the other choice?"

"Danger and disaster," Tucker replied. "The craziest of the ground-flyers used the straightaway to build up speed, because beyond the crown is a chasm. So deep, it is said, that those who did not have enough speed to reach the other side have time to die a thousand times from fright before ever reaching the bottom."

Tucker's reflective helmet turned around to watch a pair of the pod's passengers begin wild maneuvers to take them toward the platform's edge. They used the low gravity to jump high, doing backward flips and twists, the boards attached to their feet flickering like helicopter blades. Most of the boards were painted with designs to match their suits. The flyers weaved and danced, amping themselves up, preparing for the descent.

"If a flyer makes it over the chasm," Tucker went on, "the course continues all the way down to the main lock. It's a mark of prestige throughout the tunnels when someone makes it over the chasm for the first time. The trouble is, once they taste the thrill, they keep at it until they're eaten by the gorge. Lost a couple of good mates that way, I did." He observed the other flyers continue their wild antics and warned, "Do not allow them to tempt you into foolish games. Your task is to arrive, and to do so in one piece."

"Listen, it's okay, really." Rick patted the big man's arm. "Once football season was over, I used to go snowboarding every weekend."

Tucker turned back toward him. "I don't understand a word you have just said. Nor do I understand how you can be the one standing there, offering comfort to me."

"Let's go," Rick said. "I'm ready."

Tucker walked with him to the platform's edge and watched as Rick bent over and fitted his feet into the braces and tightened the straps. "How do you know how to prepare your ground-flyer?"

"I tried to tell you, I've done something like this before." Rick did not face forward, but rather stood with his front to the board's side. He straightened up, glad no one could see his grin. "A lot like it."

Another flyer hopped over and demanded, "You a first timer?"

"He doesn't need anybody's help," Abdul lashed out, moving up beside them. "He's a brave pod-fighter."

"Stay as close to the pack as you can," the flyer told him, ignoring Abdul's jibe. "There are guide markers at each side of the course, but you'll see your way clearer if you can keep up and watch what we do."

"Leave him alone, I say," Abdul snarled.

The flyer turned toward Abdul. His suit had a fanged beast painted across both back and front, with long claws reaching down over his hands and feet. "I remember another first timer," he said, his voice tinny over the suit radio. "He was so scared we had to put his board on for him. Then he had to crawl to the edge, and we all heard him scream—"

"Lies!" Abdul reached the edge with a fierce hop, grabbed hold of the rails, and launched himself high up and out. "May you . . ." The radio died to a faint hiss.

"Just keep as close to the pack as you can," the flyer told Rick. "Ready?"

"Yes," Rick said, holding back, not wanting to look over the edge until he was committed. "And thanks."

"Hey, anybody who can stay on his feet the first time he comes close to the edge is okay by me." The flyer hopped back over and joined his mates, waved once in Rick's direction, and dropped over the edge.

"I have to go." Without waiting for hesitation to slow him down, Rick took a hopping leap to the railing. The jump took him just high enough to let him have his first glimpse straight down. He gripped the rails, knowing to wait even an instant would be to freeze him solid with fear. "Thanks for coming up and seeing me off."

"Lad, you're one of the bravest—"

"Save it for the end," Rick said, and pushed himself up and over the edge.

The drop was sheer, a straight descent without any contact at all, as the cliff ducked back upon itself. Rick saw the three nearest flyers hunched over their boards, bodies twisted so as to face forward and down, one hand gripping the board's edge. Rick crouched and did the same, refusing to think of what he was actually seeing. *So far down.*

Finally the cliff moved out to greet him. With contact came sound, passing up through the board and his boots. He heard a quiet sighing as the board cruised over the super-fine silvery lunar silt. Rick passed an outcrop then and realized that the low gravity altered things mightily from what he had known before. His descent was far slower than the speeds he would have already achieved while snowboarding. He was just gradually building up speed now, even after the first long drop. And the slide did not have the same feel as a descent in higher gravity. What would have been impossible on earth was now a thrill.

The flyers before him began a series of sweeping turns, weaving back and forth in complicated patterns of joining and separating, their hands reaching out to trace finger patterns in the thick lunar dust. Rick followed suit, fashioning impossibly steep angles, almost standing upright and yet still continuing downward, his shoulder barely inches from the surface. The silt was finer than the lightest snow, streaming through his fingers like water.

It was then that he gave his first shout of joy.

The descent continued, faster and faster, the path broadening into a great sweeping bowl. At the bowl's lip was a slight rise, and the flyers ahead of him formed a single file, taking the lip in a series of great bounding leaps. Rick saw one break off to the side, slipping over the edge and simply moving into a descent, and he saw from the suit's design of purple blades that it was Abdul who had chosen not to jump.

He did not hesitate an instant. The lip swung up and he was over, leaping up higher and higher. The swooshing noise ended, no air or wind to slow him now, the only sound that of his breath. Rick looked up and saw that the transport pod hovered overhead. He waved both hands and shouted with a strength to cross the void, "This is *great!*"

He landed, pushing up a cloud of dust that shimmered like a billion tiny mirrors. Then he was beyond, swooping into the bowl and up the far side, his speed bleeding off as he crested the rise, and again there was another drop into nothing, as though the mountain had simply disappeared.

He did not hesitate, but simply launched himself forward, knowing now to grip his board's edge and raise his free hand, using it as a marksman would his gunsight, keeping himself straight and in line with the flyers up ahead.

Again the cliff came up to greet him, and he was down and running. But this time he was headed straight toward a field of huge stone fangs. The tall cliffs to either side of the run compressed like a funnel, aiming him straight for the stone spears. The razor-edged rocks crowded up to both sides of the narrowing cleft, leaving him no room whatsoever to maneuver. They looked far too tightly clustered to weave through.

Rick swallowed his sudden bile and followed the others' example, crouching low, making no turns to slow himself down, committing to a full run straight toward the rocks and their jagged knife-edges. Faster and faster until the narrowing walls became a silver-gray blur. Just as he was beginning to wonder how he would survive the impact, he saw the first of the flyers begin drifting up the cliff side, higher and higher, hanging at an impossible angle, glued to the side by speed alone.

Rick did not think, did not hesitate, did not even consider what he was about to do, just slid his weight to one side and let his board leave the silt-clad floor and begin climbing up the wall. The soft sighing was instantly replaced by a loud clattering, driving up through the soles of his boots and filling his helmet, a rattling, driving noise that seemed to push him up and up, higher on the cliff, until he was above the flint blades, then past them, then sliding back down, then swooshing back onto the floor, and screaming like a madman with the thrill.

On and on it went, his confidence growing until he was ready to move up and join the others on the straightaways, molding into their weaving patterns, mingling his shouts and half-heard cries with them. The noise rose and fell as they passed one another in their weaving dance. He obeyed their hand signals and backed off when the straightaways narrowed, watching and following their example through each of the challenging stretches.

Then they came to a straightaway that did not end, but rather broadened and continued, on and on and on. Rick knew it was the safety stretch, and part of him was beyond happy that it was almost over, while another part wished he could continue on for hours more.

Then he spotted Abdul's suit up ahead, not turning back into another sweeping curve, but rather allowing his slowing speed to lift himself up and off the stretch and onto a broad tongue of stone that flowed up and out and over the straightaway.

And Rick knew instantly what he was going to do.

The vast majority of flyers followed Abdul's example, but the flyer who had spoken with Rick swept over and shouted, "Last chance, first-timer!"

Rick did not even bother to reply.

"All *right*!" The flyer straightened from his curve, came up alongside Rick, and said, "What's your name?"

"Rick!"

"Okay, Rick, lower yourself to bring your center of gravity down . . . that's it, now start pumping. Harder. Yeah, speed's the only way, push and push, keep straight, don't let any of the speed go, hold on and push *harder*."

The voice took on a steely edge. Rick held the flyer in focus as everything else blurred into a silver-gray whirl. "That's it up ahead, ready yourself, see the ledge? Behind me, ready? Now *jump with all your might!*"

Rick did as he was told, moving in close behind the other flyer, crouching lower still, hitting the long steep ramp with such suddenness that he almost missed the chance, catching the last moment and pushing as hard as he could.

His speed was so great that on the steep rise it was harder than he expected to jump, but his adrenaline was enough to add steel to his legs, and he leapt up and out and over.

Farther and farther and farther, the jump endless, nothing below him but shadow. A darkness untouched by the stars and planet overhead, empty looming nothingness, so black it seemed to draw at him, seeking to slow him down and drag him in, never letting him go.

Just as the panic rose like bitter heat in his throat, the chasm's distant edge floated into view. The other flyer ahead screamed with the ecstasy of release. Rick held back another moment, scarcely believing he would make it to safety. Then he was so close he could see the crumbling edge, and he was still aloft, flying over and beyond and into safety, screaming himself now, landing and halting and pummeling the other flyer's back, so excited and exultant now he felt that for sure he was about ready to jump out of his own skin.

"They're not going to believe this!" the flyer crowed. "A first-timer who leaps the chasm! Don't know if it's ever been done, not even tried before. Wait till we get in, you'll have a name throughout the tunnel world."

Rick shook his head to clear the sweat pouring over his eyes. Now that it was over, his heart was pounding, his breath coming in such great gasps that he could scarcely get out the words. "I don't think I can stand."

"The weakness passes," the slender flyer assured him. "Always happens the first flight over the gorge, after you look down and know the mouth is waiting there, ready to swallow you whole."

Rick felt the words hit him square in the gut, and would have toppled had the flyer not reached out a hand to steady him. "Take a couple of deep breaths, that's it. Look around, see the stars. Ain't it great to be alive?"

Gradually his breath came under control, and strength trickled back to his shaking legs. "Great."

"Okay, steady now, time to head on back. Stand tall, now, 'cause there's a whole world who's gonna be watching you fly home."

—Nine—

Wander returned to his quarters, stripped off his robe, and collapsed onto his bed. His exhausted mind refused to slow down. Twelve hours he and Digs had remained on watch, longer than either had ever before been hooked to the amp, until even Digs had become so weak he could scarcely pull himself from the chair.

And found nothing. Six times during this past watch alone, messengers from the senior monitor had raced in, ordered them to search another sector, looking for something that was never specified.

The fifth time, Digs had lost control and screamed at the man that the nonsense was pushing them all over the edge. Either tell them what they should be hunting for, he had shouted, or let them stop.

The sixth set of orders was delivered by the watch's senior monitor, a wise old graybeard who had the power to calm the stormiest waters. He had spoken with a mildness that stilled even Digs, saying that he could not specify what to search out, because he himself had not been informed. Well, maybe the dark courier needed to be told off, Digs had said, speaking from exhaustion.

The senior monitor had hesitated at that, his silence a warning. Then he had replied simply, "Do your best."

Wander tossed in his bed, his body taut with unrelieved tension. His mind buzzed with the static of thoughts that would not come together. His heart ached with worry and with the emptiness of no outside contact. He yearned for Consuela. There had been no chance to send a message. Nor could he check to see if Consuela had left him another communication, another gift of hope. Every time he had been tempted to ask if he could reach out and check, Digs had met him with a look of desperate appeal, a fear so great that Wander knew it was wrong even to make the request.

Hope. There was so little of it. He felt as though the tension and the yearnings and the overlong watches were all mashing him down, straining out every last vestige of hope. It would be so easy to give in, to believe that the Avenger had been captured by this Hegemony-wide search, that the quest had been abandoned, that he was trapped upon Citadel for the rest of his days.

The fear of never being released, of never seeing Consuela again, threatened to snap him. He did his best to push the fog of painful loss away. But all he could manage was to keep it at arm's length, a shadow that never left him free to manage a full rest. Though his body ached with fatigue and his mind seemed stretched to the breaking point, still his worries hovered. Each time he began to descend into deep sleep, they returned to whisper and freeze his heart with nightmarish doubt. He would jerk awake, not knowing exactly why his eyes had opened but filled with the dread of hopeless longing.

Wander extinguished the lights and closed his eyes to the darkness that sought to wrap around his heart. He slid his head under the pillow and pushed with all his might against the fears. He had to rest. He had to hope. There was nothing else.

—TEN—

Consuela fitted on the headset, flicked on the amp's main switch, and watched as the chrono ticked down the seconds. Across from her, Guns and Tucker sat in alert tension, their eyes watching the chrono with her. Guns droned, "Five, four, three, two, one, now."

Instantly she powered up and sent out, *Scout here.*

Must move swiftly. There was more tension to Dunlevy's response than she could ever recall hearing before. *Have a Hegemony pilot and senior diplomat in control room. Where is Guns?*

Here. Wait. Her wrist swung down the power dial, and she said, "We have contact, but something's wrong. There's a pilot and senior diplomat there with them."

"Another dark courier." Guns rubbed his chin. "Never heard of two of them lurking about a system like this. Not without a reason."

"A major one," Tucker agreed. "Consuela, ask him if they're all right."

A relative term, Dunlevy replied, the words taut. *The captain wishes to know your status.*

"He didn't say, not really." Consuela felt Dunlevy's tension pushing at her own words. "Captain Arnol wants to know what is happening with us."

Guns and Tucker exchanged glances. At a nod from Guns, Tucker responded, "Tell him we've found passage with a caravan headed for Yalla. We're to act as outriders and guards for the cargo."

"It'll be a roundabout journey," Guns added. "They have no pilot, so we'll swing from one system to the next, following the lightways. Two planetary stops between here and there, so we should arrive within seven to ten days."

"That is," Tucker added, "unless Captain Arnol thinks this storm is going to blow over, leaving us with the chance to get back on Avenger where we belong."

Impossible, Dunlevy answered, even before Consuela had finished relating the final words. *Even as we speak, we are taking on a battalion of dragoons.*

Tucker jumped out of his seat at the news. "The Avenger's being waylaid? Why, I've a mind—"

Consuela held up one tense hand to stop him as Dunlevy continued, *I am authorized by Captain Arnol to order you to Yalla. The caravan sounds as good a cover as you are likely to find. Take it, and proceed on from there.*

But how? Consuela's heart and mind could scarcely conceal her wailing fright. *We won't be following the course we gave Wander. He won't know where to reach us, and I don't—*

No time. We're scheduled to depart in less than an hour. Tell the others we are ordered to transport the battalion back to Imperial Command. A ruse only, as they could easily have fitted on the two battleships here at Solarus spaceport. Even though they found no weapons on our ship, we are still under suspicion. Expect no further communication from us, the danger is simply too great. Dunlevy's anxiety rose another notch. *The pilot is headed this way. Get to Yalla, then hover*

*outside the planet's orbit as we said we would. We'll hope
Wander will continue to look beyond the time limits we set.
Do you still recall the system approach that he gave us?*

Yes, but—

*Then go, and may your course be true, your vision clear.
Dunlevy off.*

Consuela's numb fingers fumbled with the headset, her
hair spilling forward as she pulled it off. She looked from
one alarmed face to the other. "He's gone."

Consuela sat and listened to their planning as long as
she could, hoping they would say something to reassure
her, offer some guarantee that they would be able to renew
contact with Wander. But though they sensed her distress,
they refused to belittle her concerns or her station by offering empty words.

When sleep finally demanded her attention, she excused
herself. Guns rose with her and asked, "Would you like to
go to our place in the dome?"

"Too tired," she said simply, feeling the worry weigh
down her spirit, that and the strain of trying to filter Dunlevy's words from the continuous mental noise. "Maybe tomorrow."

Consuela moved back to the tiny alcove alongside the
storage area. There a rudimentary 'fresher abutted a row of
floor-to-ceiling bunks. She closed the door on their muted
discussion, flung herself down, and was instantly away.

Not just asleep. *Away.* No sooner had she closed her
eyes than she felt herself coming awake in that strange, eerie clarity. There, but not there. Asleep, yet awake.

Once more she faced the red-brick church, the plaza it
fronted as empty as before. Yet this time the doors were
open. They stood before her, a silent invitation. Swiftly

Consuela climbed the stairs and entered.

The preacher was already into his sermon. Consuela hesitated at the back of the hall, until the sight of two familiar faces spurred her forward. She slipped into the empty seat beside Daniel and Bliss and turned to smile at them, eager for their surprised welcome. What a wonderful gift of reassurance, she thought, to bring her back for a church service with her oldest friends.

But it did not come. Daniel remained as he was, his face turned intently toward the pulpit. Bliss sat on his other side, cradling one of Daniel's hands in both of hers, as intent on the pastor's words as her husband. Consuela sighed her way back around, disappointed that she was unable to make them realize she was there, yet happy just the same for this gift of comfort. At least she could sit here beside her friends and hear the pastor offer her encouragement.

But it was not to be.

"Be ready," the pastor was saying. "For we know not the day nor the hour. How many times have we heard these words? So often, I would imagine, that we have all but lost the ability to look beyond the clearest message, that of hoping for our Savior's return, and see what else might be there . . . what other message might be intended."

There it was again. *Be ready*. Consuela felt a rising sense of resentment. She was hurting, she was worried, she needed assurance that all would work out as she hoped. But instead, what was she hearing? A challenge. A call to do more. Her first reaction was to turn away, simply stand up and walk out. She did not need this. Not now. Yet something held her there, a quiet whisper beyond the borders of sound, spoken to her heart. A plea to remain, to listen, to learn, to *grow*.

"More than likely, every one of us has arrived at some point or another where we have turned to God and asked,

Why is this happening? Where are we going? What is the purpose here?" He paused to gaze around the chamber. "Remember, now, the Lord has not promised to always lift us from trouble. Instead, He said that He would *be there with us*.

"So long as we are upon this earth, we shall know trials. But by bearing up under this burden, by showing the world that we meet these stresses and strains as Christians, we are granted the chance to become beacons. To show others, who continue to suffer in the darkness, that we have a gift of hope to share.

"Now think about what this means. God does not say, first I will make your lives perfect, and then ask you to go out and save the world. Not at all. He says, abide in me, and I in you, and be my servant. Where you are. Right now.

"Then you will be able to listen for the words that our Savior yearns to hear, using your ears and your heart and your mind and voice as His own. People may cry from their lonely darkness, I am confused. I am lost. Where am I going? Why I am being forced to turn down this strange road with all its pains and perils? And you, my brothers and sisters, can say give to them the gifts of grace. The peace that surpasses understanding. A light that pierces the darkest night. A love that heals the greatest sorrow. As you yourselves have come to know."

He stopped then and seemed to look straight at Consuela, as though he and only he was able to see her. As though his words were intended for her. For *her*.

"Therefore, my brothers and sisters, *be ready*. It may be this very moment that the Lord is trying to gain your attention, to ask you to do as you have been commanded and allow His infinite strength to bear your burdens, and *be ready*. Be ready to listen. Be ready to speak. Be ready to *serve*."

–Eleven–

By the time the caravan arrived at the last stop before Yalla, Rick was beyond bored.

The merchant's son, Abdul, was chief of caravan security. He had responded to their presence by emptying the very back hold and ordering them all inside. He had then welded shut the only door leading to the remainder of the caravan, then sealed them even tighter with restrictions. No radio communication of any sort. No sorties outside the hold, unless the alarm was raised. No trial sorties whatsoever. Guns and Tucker had argued directly with Mahmut that the restrictions left them hamstrung and unable to do their duty. But Mahmut chose not to overrule his son, and they were left isolated and confined.

Upon his arrival, Rick had flown the caravan's length. It looked like a colossal floating junkyard. Vessels of every size and description were bolted together with thick steel girders. Thruster units jutted from long steel arms at odd intervals. It had seemed to Rick that the merchant had bought whatever had come cheap, then attached it wherever there was room. The result was a massive metal spacebound bug, as ugly as it was huge.

Most of the troopers were seasoned enough to know the universal pattern of soldiering—hours of boredom followed by seconds of sheer terror. They gambled and gossiped and lounged, storing food and sleep in limitless amounts. Rick had little money to begin with, and soon had none. He spent as much time as he could making dry runs on the Blade's weapons system. By the time they made their second halt at yet another minor system, the weapons fitted to him like a glove.

When not working in the Blade, Rick retreated to a private corner for quiet reflection. It was a hard activity, and one which seemed to do little more than bore holes in his confidence. But still it held him, as though there were actually some purpose behind his forced detachment. Their chamber was extensive, with numerous nooks and crannies that were quickly claimed by other troopers seeking a bit of solitude. He had chosen for himself a perch halfway up the side wall, an aerie from which he could view their metal-bound world.

"Rick?"

The unexpected voice made him jump. Consuela continued up the wall-rungs until her head came into view. "May I join you?"

"Sure." He pushed his bedding to one side, then slid over to make room for her.

"Thanks." She sank down beside him, looked out and over the edge, and said, "This is nice."

"It's okay, I guess."

She pointed down to where Tucker was loading his troopers into the transport. "Are you going with them?"

"I can't," he replied glumly. "They only let one pod out at each landing. My number didn't come up."

She nodded her understanding. When the caravan entered a parking orbit, Tucker and his men landed with the caravan's own transport and guarded during the off-load-ing. This much Mahmut had insisted upon, overriding his son's strident objections that their own men were suffi-cient. "From what I've heard," Consuela said, "you're not missing much. Tucker said the last landing was on a place so dinky he'd never even heard of it."

"What about you?" Rick asked. "Doesn't it bother you, not being let out of this cage for a week?"

She shook her head and confessed, "I've been too wor-ried about Wander."

"You still can't raise him?"

"I can't *try*." Frustration creased her forehead. "I'm not a trained pilot. Even if I knew where he was, I couldn't ex-tend myself out there to some invisible pathway and lay down a message. I can't even find the place."

"What about Dunlevy?"

"I'm worried about him too. And Captain Arnol. There hasn't been any word from them since we left Solarus. They know our course."

"Maybe Dunlevy tried and missed you."

"I doubt it. I haven't done much besides sit at the con-sole." She hesitated, then added, "That and pray."

The softly spoken word shook Rick to the core. It felt as though all the time and all the solitude had been pushing and prodding, preparing him for that moment, so that when it came, he would be open. Able to reach beyond his pride and confess, "I've been doing a lot of thinking. About home, and myself. Where I'm going, what I'm supposed to do."

Her gaze held the calm of one ready to listen for hours. "Do you want to go back?"

"I don't *know*." All the frustration and confusion of the past eight days boiled over. "It's crazy. I've got everything I could possibly ask for here. I love this life and the adventure, but something, I don't . . ." Rick let his voice trail off.

She waited until she was sure he couldn't finish for himself, then said softly, "Something is missing."

It welled up within him like a vast emotional bubble rising to the surface of his thoughts. As though just waiting for a time like this, for him to acknowledge, "All the success and excitement I've been having, it's as though I've been painting over something. A hollowness inside. And now, when I'm forced to sit here on my hands, I can't help but see that it's still there." He shrugged helplessly. "So I've been wondering if maybe I need to go back. Like maybe I'm not supposed to be here."

"Maybe what you're supposed to do is ask for guidance," Consuela said quietly.

There was something in her voice, a depth of understanding that made him feel ashamed to think of how he had tried to pressure her into a relationship. As though here in this rusty hold, her tender intensity was inviting him to a level of trust and friendship he had never known before. "Ask God, you mean?"

She nodded. "Maybe it's not the place or the activity that is the problem. But what you're doing it *for*."

Rick felt a harmony with her words, so strong it resounded through his being like the pealing of a great bell. The force shattered his shield of pride, leaving him free to admit, "That makes sense."

"Hard as it is to bow our heads," Consuela went on, as though understanding his deepest thoughts, "maybe that's what is called for here. To accept that without the Lord, we are nothing, just empty vessels going through the motions of life. We need to confess our weaknesses, our sins, our emptiness. And turn our lives over to Him."

Our *weaknesses*. Again there was the sense of resounding force, so strong Rick was able to see and understand

and say, "I feel like all my life I've had to be the strong one. Make the family look good. Do everything just right. Be on top."

"And all the while," Consuela offered softly, "hold inside everything that did not fit with the image. Every doubt, every failing, every weakness."

He nodded, his chest suddenly burning with the freedom of confession. "I didn't even let *myself* see those things."

"But they were still there." Her own gaze turned inward, able to understand because she had confronted the same truth within herself. "Making every success empty, turning every triumph into a lie."

They shared a long silence, one filled with a power as comforting as it was real. Finally Consuela said, "Would you like to pray with me?"

—Twelve—

As Consuela and Rick descended to the hold's floor, Guns came bounding toward them. "There you are, good. Need to speak with you both."

He started to usher them over to one side, but halted to watch the transport return and ground. When the portal unsealed, Tucker was the first to hop from the transport. His hands gripped two carry-sacks of purchased provisions, and his expression was dour. "A more miserable rock I have never set my feet on, and hope never to again." He raised one sack and shook it toward Guns. "Do you know what they wanted to charge me for simple bread?"

"It doesn't matter," Guns said impatiently. "We—"

"It may not matter to you, matey," Tucker said, still venting steam. "But I'll be switched if a flour-dusted thief is going to make off with my hard-earned gold. Not without a fight, he won't."

Guns planted hands on wiry hips. "Are you done?"

"Aye, I suppose so." Tucker tossed his sacks to a waiting trooper. "What's got you in a lather?"

"While you were off gallivanting, we had ourselves a visitor."

"One thing for certain, matey, there was little gallivanting going on by us or anyone else on that gloomy world."

"Listen up, will you? While Abdul went down with your lot, the father came a-calling."

"Old Mahmut showed up, did he?" Tucker was vastly unimpressed. "I hope you told him we were going stir crazy in this tiny tin room."

"I did," Guns crowed, "and he said our waiting was over."

Rick and Tucker exclaimed together, "What?"

"Aye, I thought that would get a rise out of you." Guns grinned wolfishly. "It turns out, Mahmut let his son have his way only because our route up to now was pretty safe. The lightways we've been following have been almost totally empty routes, touching down on secondary planets."

"Secondary is far too kind, if you ask me," Tucker interjected.

"But it makes sense," Rick exclaimed, the thought of possible freedom agitating his words. "That would also explain why Consuela's not spotted a shadowlane, much less any pirate activity."

"Aye, the lad has a point," Tucker agreed grudgingly, as though reluctant to let go of his irritation. One of Consuela's constant responsibilities had been to search the way ahead, extending the tiny training amp to its limit, checking to see if there was any trace of a shadowlane.

"But here our course joins the most heavily traveled route in Vector Nine," Guns went on, his eyes sparking with excitement. "And there have been four ships gone missing in the last twenty days that he knows of."

"You don't say," Tucker murmured.

"Apparently caravans coming in to purchase these firestones on Yalla are full to the brim with trading goods. Not to mention the fact that a half-dozen routes all converge at this point," Guns continued. "Only reason this system is inhabited."

"Which means there are planet-bound eyes and ears just looking for news of rich pickings to pass on to the pirates," Tucker said.

Guns crossed his arms, his grin fierce. "Now tell me what those very same spies heard your boys grumbling about while they were down on that forsaken planet."

"Nothing much," Tucker said, returning the grin. "Just how they'd been hired and then crammed in a hold, left to sit on their hands."

"Just what I thought. Mahmut may not have realized it, but by keeping us in the dark, and giving our boys a reason to complain, he just might have let us set ourselves up for some action." Guns turned his gaze toward Rick. "Assemble the outriders. I think this news is too good to keep to ourselves."

"Right," Rick said, and bolted.

Tucker asked, "Does this mean you can get out there and train?"

"As much as we like," Guns replied. "Not to mention station outriders as we see fit."

"I imagine our little friend Abdul will fair explode," Tucker predicted, "when he hears his father is lifting the restrictions."

"Aye, it pains me that I won't be able to listen in on that discussion," Guns agreed, and turned to Consuela. "The practice runs are over, lass. We need you to be reaching out as far and wide as you can."

"I understand," Consuela affirmed. "Search out the shadowlanes and see if there are any pirates lying in wait."

"Same as you've been doing so far," Guns confirmed. "Only now, if what Mahmut says is true, this run is for real."

$-$ THIRTEEN $-$

Rick bent over her sleeping form, reached out an arm, and hesitated. She looked so fragile, so tired, and yet so beautiful. Her hair was scattered over the pillow, as dark as her long eyelashes, making her skin look porcelain pure. It was strange, how he could look down at her now, and feel his heart twist at the fragile strength, and be content to be her friend. As though all the storm of conflicting emotions was suddenly gone, leaving him free to look and examine himself first, and others afterward, with an honesty he had never known before.

She stirred, rolling over, and he touched her shoulder. "Consuela, it's time."

"It can't be," she murmured, not opening her eyes. "I just lay down."

"Four hours ago," he said.

"Your chrono is off." She rolled back over. "Bye."

"Guns says to tell you that by his best estimate, we've already passed beyond the farthest point of your last search." When she did not move, he had to smile. "He also said he was brewing up one of his special cups, just for you."

"That's not fair." She drew the covers up over her head.

He felt for her, knew from the circles under her eyes that she needed a longer, deeper rest. But there was no alternate for her watch. Mahmut had informed Guns that he was doubling his normal rate of acceleration, burning fuel at a prodigious level in order to pass through this hazardous region as swiftly as possible. Rick urged, "We need you."

She sighed her way back out from under the covers, opened her eyes, and managed a tired smile. "I was having the nicest dream."

The look in her eye told him all. "About Wander?"

She nodded, suddenly shy. "He didn't say anything. He just looked at me. And smiled. For a moment it was as though he was here with me." She looked at him. "Does it bother you, that I talk about him like this?"

He searched his heart and answered honestly, "Not anymore."

She brought the world and his face into clearer focus. "Have you been thinking about what we discussed?"

"And praying," Rick replied. "It feels nice. More than that. It feels *right*."

"I'm glad, Rick. Really, really glad." She rubbed her face and said, "Pray for me too, will you? Most of the time I feel so weak, and Wander seems so far away."

"It's going to turn out fine," he said, and for once truly believed his own words.

A few moments later she emerged from the 'fresher, accepted the cup from Guns with a smile, and entered the transport. As always whenever she was standing duty, a pair of troopers came to lounge around the portal. The chance of anyone entering from the caravan and spying her operating the portable console were slim. But it was a chance they could not afford to take.

It seemed as though she had scarcely had time to power

up before her shrill cry brought all activity within the hold to an absolute halt. Rick raced over, a half step behind Tucker and Guns, in time to see her emerge from the portal. Her hair was disheveled from her having ripped off the headset, her eyes were frantic. "They're *here!*"

"How far," Guns rapped out.

"Here," she repeated, her voice almost a scream. "Right ahead, not seconds—"

"Blades!" Guns was already running for his pod. "Red alert! Power up!"

"Troopers! By me!" Tucker's voice roared across the hold. "Grab your suits and to the transport! Flight Lieutenant, power up!"

Rick raced across the hold to his pod and tore his sleeve from shoulder to elbow in his scramble through the plasteel hole. He shouted the order to close the Blade's entry platform and started running through the power sequence even before he was fully settled in the seat. Even so, when he looked up and through the front screen, Guns was already up and headed for the portal.

"Knight Two here," Rick said, glad that his voice was crisp despite the thunder of his heart, gladder still to hear two more Blades counting out behind him.

"You heard the lass," Guns said, leading them though the first translucent energy-plate and then the second and into space, powering forward as soon as they were clear. Rick was tight on his tail. "They're right around here some—"

"Bandits at three o'clock high!" Rick cried, his voice rising a full octave at the sight of the dull black surface glinting in the starlight.

"Shields to full power!" Guns sped forward, clearing the front edge of the caravan. "Attack on my—"

Then the endless night of space was shattered by flickering stun bolts. Purple lances hit the ship at a half-dozen points, the secondary force burning out in evil-colored lightning. One of the Blade flyers shrieked in Rick's ears, caught by an aftershock. Rick craned and saw the stone-covered pod go careening off.

"Conform to me," Guns snapped. "I've marked his trajectory. All right, it's up to us and us alone. I'm going for their power, Blade Three—"

A second voice shrilled, "Transports peeling off, three, no four, I count four headed this way. Attack pods to either side!"

"They're mine!" Rick headed straight for the unsuspecting invaders.

"Blade Six here, I'm with you."

"Right." Guns' voice held the sharp clarity of a seasoned warrior. "The rest with me, fire together, go for their weapons, count down from five, four, three, two, one, *now*."

Three of the enemy pods spotted their fire and peeled off toward them. Rick roared with the adrenaline surge of coming battle and powered up his energy lance.

"Four here, the enemy's primary vessel was only partially hit. Their defenses seem to be holding."

Rick's attention remained fixed upon the nearest attack pod. The instant his energy lance was activated, his Blade's stony cover exploded outward, shattering in a million bits, leaving the Blade exposed for all to see. The pod tried to veer, but from the sluggish response Rick knew it was radio controlled. Where the flyer should have sat was filled with a larger energy pack and more weaponry. But the pod had chance to use neither, for Rick flew in at full power, raging straight through the attacker and heading for the second.

"Aye, they were alerted, no question, prepare to receive incoming fire." Guns' voice was a fiery roar. "Evasion tactics and fire at will!"

A second cannon bolt seared the space nearby, temporarily blinding Rick, the immensity of the power telling him he was drawing fire from the mother ship. Through the dancing sparks in his vision he spotted smaller flickerings of energy bolts; though he could no longer see the pod, he headed straight for the source of the smaller fire and knew he had struck home when a grinding, rending crash filled his small cabin.

"*Get that cannon,*" Guns roared. "They may go for the caravan!"

"Can't," came a breathless reply. "Winged me, lost tracking."

"Their defenses are strongest around the weapon," came another voice. "I've hit it twice straight on."

"Do it again!"

"More pods! Out the aft portal, six, no seven!"

"Forget the pods. *Hit that cannon.*"

"I'm going in!" Before he could reflect upon what he was going to try, Rick switched all power to his lance and forward shields. His rear totally exposed to fire from the attack pods, Rick swerved away from the dogfight and aimed straight for the mother ship and its deadly ring of weaponry.

The blaster cannons formed a circle of malignant snouts halfway down the ship's length. One swiveled about and began tracking him. Instantly he swerved, but not far, because it was only straight ahead that he was protected. The cannon fired, but his visor was down, and instead of being temporarily blinded, he saw how the near miss outlined his forward shield, now extended almost as far as the energy lance itself, layer after layer of cover, a series of golden lances formed one within the next. Rick took heart from the sight, hunched his shoulders, and powered straight for the ship.

There was a great shrill shrieking as the two shields met, a squeal so high he felt it more than heard it. His skull hummed like a tuning fork, his vision blurred, and for a moment of sheer panic he thought he had failed, that the Blade would shatter from the rending force. Then he was through, and the first cannon was chopped apart by his lance, then the second, the space now filled with spinning fragments of molten metal, the air in his cabin swollen with the crashing clamor.

He continued around the ship in his destructive circle, the cannons ahead firing in futile fury, the energy bolts shooting out in every direction, unable to strike him. One by one the snouts fell like great metal trees until the circle was complete and the space about the mother ship was littered with ruddy red bits of steel. And the cannons were silent.

The mopping-up procedures were swift and sure. Under Guns' command, all their fire was directed aft to the thrusters, which soon glowed fiery red, and melted into a sullen heap. At that point the remaining attack pods traversed to the pirate transports and attached themselves in silent surrender. The two wounded Blades were returned to the hold, lines were attached to both the mother ship and the invading transports, then Guns rapped out, "Going to open channel." There was a short pause, then, "Senior outrider calling the Merchant Ahmet and his Caravan Desert Queen."

There was a long moment of silence, then through the hiss came a feeble voice. "Desert Queen here. Our flight deck took a direct hit, we surrender. Repeat, we surrender. Don't shoot."

"No need, laddie, the pirates beat you to it," Guns replied, a glint of dry humor coming through. "The bandits have been routed. We are sounding the all clear. Repeat, all clear."

There was a longer silence, then a very weak Mahmut himself came on and demanded hoarsely, "Can this be?"

"Just tell us where you want us to deposit the raiders," Guns replied, "and you can see for yourself."

—Fourteen—

"Firestones are more than a simple jewel," Mahmut explained. "For some, it is almost a religion."

Tucker shifted his weight on the cushion, and instantly Guns was alongside. "You all right, matey?"

"Just slide that pad up a notch, will you?" Tucker grimaced as Guns eased him more upright. The big man had been stepping into the transport when the stun bolt had struck, and he had fallen hard, straining his back. "That's better, Guns. Thanks."

"I shall have my personal physician attend to you again tomorrow," Mahmut promised. "He reports that the massage has helped ease your discomfort."

"Aye, perhaps," Tucker reluctantly allowed. "But I can't say as I enjoyed the experience."

"You made enough noise," Rick observed.

"Seems a bit strange," Guns agreed, "a big fellow like you, being bested by an old fellow who couldn't hardly weigh as much as a wet breeze."

"I'd like to see how well you manage," Tucker blustered. "That man has fingers of solid titanium."

"Easy, mate, I didn't mean anything by it," Guns said

with a grin. "Anyway, it's good to see you up and about again."

"That it is," Mahmut agreed. He raised his cup and said for the dozenth time that night, "A toast to the gallant warriors and their magnificent victory."

Since their return from the battle, all had changed within the caravan. The portal had been unsealed, and they had all been granted free reign of the ship. Mahmut had loaded them all down with gifts and declared that all money from the sale of the pirate vessel was theirs and theirs alone.

They were seated in Mahmut's private quarters, a sumptuous chamber lined with brilliantly colored tapestries and luxurious carpets of intricate design. They rested upon ample silk cushions, and before each person stood an individual hand-carved table, laden with goblets of filigreed silver and the remnants of a grand feast.

Guns stretched out his legs and asked, "How's your son getting on?"

"He rests easy, and the doctor promises that there will be no permanent damage," Mahmut replied. A flicker of concern passed over his features. "If it had not been for your swift actions—"

"A stun bolt can knock the best of men for a loop," Guns said, doing away with the need for more thanks. "You were saying something about those firestones of Yalla."

"Of Yalla, indeed." It was Mahmut's turn to lean back, settle himself, and stroke his slender beard. Dark eyes moved from one guest to the next. "Do I perhaps detect more of an interest in Yalla than just that of mercenaries seeking their next posting?"

"We are honest men," Guns protested. "There'll be no thieving—"

Tucker cut him off with, "That's not what the merchant is on about, matey."

"Indeed." The eyes continued to probe each of his four guests in turn—Tucker, Guns, Rick, and finally Consuela. They lingered long upon her, until he said, "You will forgive me for saying how strange it seems, that at the banquet to celebrate the victors, you choose to include a young lady who only today has regained her strength."

"I'm fine," Consuela said, misunderstanding him. And she was. She had powered down, but remained at the console with the damping headset in place in case they wanted her to search farther out. Instead, when the stun bolt struck, the headset had the effect of damping out much of the bolt's effect. She had experienced the mental agony of a harsh electric shock but had not lost consciousness, and had been one of the first to recover. "Really."

"I am delighted to hear this," Mahmut said gravely. "And yet, still I fail to understand what grand role you have played in our rescue from the pirates."

Tucker and Guns exchanged worried glances before Tucker responded, "That's our secret."

Mahmut gave a grave nod. "And I, in turn, am not in a position to refuse you anything. Yet I must warn you that if I tell you all that I know of these firestones and of Yalla itself, my life and all my possessions would be delivered into your hands."

"You want an exchange of secrets," Guns said slowly, "to know you can trust us."

"Family honor *requires* that I trust you now," Mahmut countered. "But the pirates, they will not stop with this one attack. I am not insisting, and yet, as a merchant plying the hazards of space, I would ask to know what your secret is."

Guns and Tucker exchanged a second, longer look, before Tucker finally nodded and said, "Fire away."

Guns turned back, sighed, and said, "We can only tell you what secrets are ours to share."

Dark eyes widened in surprise. "Mercenaries who carry the secrets of others?"

"We're not," Tucker said quietly, "what you might consider your ordinary run-of-the-mill mercenaries."

"The lass here," Guns said, "is what they call a Talent."

The merchant's eyes became round in astonishment. "The legends come alive, one after another. First the pirates become more than myth, and now a Sensitive shares my table."

"You hold more than our lives in your hands," Tucker warned.

"By the head of my only son, these are secrets I shall share with none other," Mahmut promised.

Guns turned to Consuela and said, "Tell him."

So she explained the shadowlanes and the pattern of searching down the lightways. Mahmut listened in a silence so focused and intense that she could literally feel the strength of his gaze upon her. When she stopped, he sat and sipped from his goblet, digesting the information, before turning to Guns and asking, "And these remarkable attack pods of yours?"

"That," Guns replied, "is not our secret to share."

"Someone has equipped you to hunt down pirates," Mahmut breathed.

Guns and Tucker responded with faces of stone.

"I understand," Mahmut said, and set down his goblet. "Very well. It is now my turn.

"Among merchant caravans, Yalla is known as the impenetrable world," Mahmut began. "It is a world of secrets and levels. I have known success there only because my mother was a Yalla native, from a chieftain's family. She fell in love with a merchant trader, my father, and agreed to exchange the desert reaches for his life of spacing. Because of this, I have been granted leave to sit at the edge of the tribal fires and share in the bounty of firestones. Only a handful of traders carry the gems, and fewer still are ever permitted to land. Lifetimes have been spent transporting wares to Yalla and shipping the gems away, without once setting foot upon the golden sands."

"Why the secrecy?" Guns demanded.

"Ah, the mystery. Yes." Another sip to fortify himself, and then, "You understand, to say more places all that I have in your hands."

"We have already shown you," Guns said, "that we can both be trusted, and hold our secrets well."

"It is as you say." Mahmut leaned forward and said with quiet intensity. "It is said that the firestones do not come from Yalla at all, but rather from another system entirely. One so mysterious that no record of its existence remains anywhere."

Guns did not even notice that he spilled his goblet as he catapulted to the front of his cushion. "What?"

"Ah, I see that this interests you. Yes, this rumor has never even been whispered to me, one who has spent a lifetime trading for the Yalla chieftains, and who has traced his way through the secret caverns since he was able to walk. But I have learned the ability to sift through the sands of time and desert, and capture the hidden meanings. A word here, a shrug there, and over the years I have come to believe that this is why the chieftains are so reluctant to allow any visitor to set foot upon their globe. Because, in truth, there is nothing there."

"You don't say," Tucker breathed.

"Why else," the merchant continued, "would there be great dunes hollowed out, to conceal fleets of small, swift-running craft?"

"For planetary defense?" Guns hedged.

"Perhaps," Mahmut conceded. "And yet, not even the Hegemony is granted much leave upon Yalla. Firestones are coveted by the dark couriers, and it said that the emperor himself has been known to lose himself within the cabalism of firestone worship."

Consuela exchanged a glance with Rick, saw him blanch at the words. Guns said for them all, "Sounds a strange way for the ruler of all the Hegemony to conduct himself."

"My mother made me swear never to handle a polished firestone," Mahmut replied. "So I can say nothing from experience. But I hear from others that it is a rite as addictive as any drug."

"So the Imperium leaves the planet alone," Guns suggested. "These gems or whatever they are, they're too valuable to risk cutting off their supply."

"So do I think," Mahmut agreed. "And the tribes have spent centuries perfecting the art of guarding secrets."

"Have you ever," Tucker demanded, "heard the name of this hidden world?"

"There was once a word spoken," Mahmut replied, his voice dropping to a whisper. "A word murmured in the late of night, by one so old he did not realize what it was he said. After that night, I never saw the elder again." Mahmut looked from one face to the next, then finished, "The word was Citadel."

–FIFTEEN–

Tucker followed her across the oasis, back toward the cavern entrance and their transport, and asked once more, "Are you sure you want to keep this up?"

"I have to." Consuela massaged her neck with one hand, more tired than she had ever been in her life. "There's no other hope, is there?"

"Even so, lass, you've set yourself a killing schedule."

"It's not that bad," she insisted, trying for a light tone. But her voice sounded flat and drained even to her ears, and her eyes were gritty with more than just the desert sands. "All I do is sit behind the console."

"Anybody who looks at you knows you can't go on like this much longer," Tucker replied worriedly. "And without you we have no hope of finding him, lass. None at all."

Consuela had been resting beyond the last trees, where tall flat stones acted as a natural break-wall against the desert winds. Before her had stretched endless waves of golden sand, rising and falling in sweeping ridges to the distant horizon. Now as she walked back toward the looming entrance, a trio of ruddy peaks rose to her right. Other than these three lonely mountains, the desert reached out boundless and forbidding. Under the utterly empty sky, the setting sun glowed huge and orange, as though it were melting into the sands.

Already by this fifth day on Yalla, they had formed the habit of going aloft for the day's final hour. This was the hour of calm, so named because the heat and the fierce winds of day had dimmed, and the cold winds of night had not yet begun. One of the elders had told them at the feast marking their arrival that Yalla had a second name among its desert folk. They called it "The Place of Storms."

Consuela shivered at the memory of their arrival, the heat and huge sun and triple moons, the wind and lightning and desert sands. From the portal in Mahmut's quarters she had watched their descent and felt as though she were diving into a boiling yellow sea.

When they had passed the system's second gas giant, the ones that the ship Avenger had been intended to mine, a trio of Yalla battleships had arrived to escort them forward. Tucker and Guns had told Mahmut they would have preferred to stay aloft in the caravan, but the trader had nervously requested that they descend. He said that the tribesmen wanted to formally thank the ones who had saved one of their own from the pirates. Then he had drawn them aside and explained that the chieftains did not want to have leaders of such a strong fighting force out in space, and that even he and his son would be required to remain in their custody until negotiations and off-loading were completed. Never before had strangers been made welcome on Yalla, Mahmut had told them. Clearly the desert warriors were worried about allowing the leaders of such fighters to remain overhead, circling their planet.

Tucker and Guns had reluctantly agreed, then watched as Yalla guard pods came to station themselves about the caravan. A suspicious lot, was all Mahmut had said. If you want to keep your pods a secret, make sure your troopers stay on the alert, and weld your hold-doors shut.

Now as Consuela approached the vast cave entrance with its decorations of burnished metal and intricate carvings, the sun disappeared below the horizon. Almost instantly the first night winds began blowing their chill whispers of coming cold. Consuela shivered again, wanting to stay out of the stone-lined hall, knowing she had to go in.

"Aye, back where I come from, they'd call this a lazy wind," Tucker said, leading her around the last stand of stumpy trees, their short height sheltered from the worst of the storms by the ring of stone guarding the cavern entrance. "It can't be bothered to go around you, so it just blows straight through."

"You've never said anything about where you are from."

"That's because there isn't much to say." He nodded to the portal guard, who ignored them entirely. Since the feast marking their arrival, the desert clan had not spoken a single word to any of them. Even so, with each day the air of resentment over their presence grew stronger. The desert soldier was dressed in traditional garb of robe and hood and cloak against the coming night, his blaster slung across his back. "The best thing I can say about my homeworld is I'm not there anymore."

"Do you ever miss your family?" Consuela entered between the tall stone pillars carved from the rock entrance and rising up to five times her height. The portal was large enough for even the caravan's transport to have entered through, and was flanked by a pair of great iron doors.

"My mother passed over while I was still a lad. My father was a good man, but he married again, and his second wife preferred her own children to the one from his first wife. She wasn't sorry to see the back of me." They proceeded across the entrance hall, a cavern that dwarfed the transports nestled at their center. Only one of the tribes-men they passed even looked their way, and that was to pierce Consuela with a look of bitter hostility.

This first cavern was as far into the tribe's underground hive as they had been permitted to enter. They skirted around the caravan's transport, a vessel large enough to contain both a residence for Mahmut and a large cargo hold. Beyond both rested their one guard pod, which remained encased within its plasteel shell. This was the pod that had been struck by the stunner and kept out of the battle. They had decided to leave the plasteel cover in place for precisely such a time as this. Rick waved to her from his station at the pod's base. One of Mahmut's most trusted personal guards kept him company. None of their own troopers had been permitted to land.

Tucker walked her over to their transport's portal and asked once more, "Are you sure you want to do this?"

"I have to," Consuela replied, and cut off further argument by entering the transport and shutting the portal.

She had spent every waking hour at the mind amp, even taking her meals at the console. Sleep had come in snatches, her dreams often ending in a burst of fear that she had missed a take-off, and thus lost her only opportunity to follow the tribal fleet to Citadel. In truth, she had not really rested for five days now, and the strain was wearing her down.

She fitted on the headset, powered up, closed her eyes, and began yet another search around the desert planet. The practice had become almost second nature now, sweeping out and around with growing confidence.

The space around Yalla was utterly silent, for the planet possessed neither true spaceport nor watch communicator. The desert chieftains preferred to keep themselves and their secrets under close control, and there was too great a risk that any communicator trained by the Hegemony would be an Imperial spy.

The first signal was so unexpected that she almost missed it.

Then it came again, startling her so that when she tried to bolt upright, she tumbled from her chair, ripping the headset from her temples. She gave a panic-stricken cry and righted herself. She struggled to refit the headset, her fingers made clumsy with haste.

Tucker clanged open the portal and demanded, "Is everything—"

Frantically she waved him to silence, hunched so far over that her forehead touched her knees. Her eyes were so tightly shut she saw stars. Consuela hunted, hunted, then quietly, the words almost a moan, "I've found strange ships."

Tucker moved with stealth, shut the portal, slid the bolts home. "You're sure?"

"Four of them," she whispered, wishing he would listen, say nothing, simply let her focus and use his silent strength as an anchor. "The size of our transport, no bigger."

"Then their destination can't be too far off."

"They're making course out of the system." For an instant she opened her eyes, fearful of what was to come, searching for the here and now. "But there's no lightway."

"Follow them, lass," Tucker hissed, crouching down beside her, reaching out a tentative hand, withdrawing it before making contact. "It's our only chance."

"I don't . . ." Consuela felt a tremor of fear course through her. Already the ships were reaching out beyond the system's limits, with nothing but black and empty space surrounding them.

"*Follow,*" he urged.

She sighed her way back down, one hand to her forehead, the other reaching out to be swallowed by Tucker's massive grip. She stayed with the ships. Fighting off the terror of uncharted space, refusing to worry that the return would be impossible, that she might stop and turn about and find herself lost, alone, to hurl forever in panic-stricken search for refuge. She offered a swift prayer for guidance, and gave herself over fully to the challenge.

The Yalla transporters continued to gain speed, streaming an energy trail far behind, burning fuel at an alarming pace. She watched them continue to accelerate at their punishing rate, then, "They've vanished."

"N-space," Tucker breathed. "And so fast. Either they've a pilot aboard—"

"No," she said, definite on that point, while still remaining outward focused and searching, though the terror of having no fixed point upon which to fasten threatened to swallow her whole.

"—Then they've got a system close at hand, and they know the jump backward and forward, so much they can make do with a line sight and old records." Tucker hesitated, then asked, "Do you see a system dead ahead of where they were last?"

"Yes. One of the closest to us."

"Go there."

"It's not that easy. I can't—"

"Do it, lass." His grip tightened. "For your Wander."

At the sudden sound of his name, she flung herself out, her hand on the console sweeping the power control up to the limit, not pausing an instant for thought, just going.

And colliding straight into the strongest focus of mind-amp power she had ever known.

Not directed toward her. Not yet. The force inundated space about the planet like a multitude of brilliant lighthouse beams, all directed far outward, searching, searching.

Again there was no time for thought. She did not need to inspect. She *knew*. Wander was *there*. She drew back a fraction and bundled together all the anxieties, all the yearnings, all the frustrations and fatigues and longings from those endless fearful days. She wrapped them with the cords of her growing love, shimmering bonds of heartsong, and *flung* them toward the planet. And in the same instant, though she longed to stay and see if they were received, she retreated. A leap across the limitless chasm of emptiness, wishing she could stay, wishing she could shout his name to the heavens, knowing to do so would draw down doom upon their heads, praying with all her heart that he would hear, and understand.

She raised up with an effort, opened her eyes, and found a round-eyed Tucker watching her with burning intensity. She nodded once and managed, "It's there."

–Sixteen–

The platform carrying Wander and the other watch monitors descended into utter bedlam.

The monitors riding the platform down were completely silent. They hung over the side rails, their faces blanching with each wail rising from below. As the platform approached the cavern's floor, figures began springing from their positions and racing over.

The senior monitor riding the platform waved those below back to their stations and screamed, "You're all going on report!" There were three senior monitors, one for each watch. Like all personnel, their own watches and subordinates had become hopelessly scrambled. The senior monitor leaned over the railing and shouted down, "Back to your stations!"

Someone down below shrilled, "We're being attacked!" As the platform sank to the cavern's floor, several distraught faces came in line with Wander's. Their eyes showed white all around. "Something is coming!"

Another voice within the milling throng yelled, "It's not coming, it's here!"

As soon as the railing dropped, two monitors shoved

their way onto the platform. More panic-stricken figures came streaming from the mind-amps. One cried, "Get me out of here!"

"Back, I say!" Bony arms protruded from the senior monitor's robes as he tried to stop the charge by will alone. The senior monitor travelling upon the platform was thoroughly disliked. He was far older than the other senior monitors, and not up to the crisis at hand. He covered this by sudden outbursts and constant criticism. "Remember your duties!"

"I am hereby on sick leave," a monitor declared, shoving his way onto the platform. "I've done more than enough overtime to sleep my way through the rest of this."

One of those just arriving demanded, "What was it?"

"I don't know and I don't want to know."

"Did anyone else hear anything?"

"I didn't need to," came the reply. "I've had all I can take of this balderdash."

"I heard someone cry out," another offered.

Two more crowded their way on. One of them agreed, "It came from the mind-amp next to ours. Stood my hair on end, I can tell you that." From the safety of the platform, he glanced about and said, "Where are they?"

His compatriot replied, "Sprawled in the dust at the foot of their station."

The senior monitor whirled about, grasping at the robes of several scouts who were pressing themselves upon the platform. Then he realized that none of those who had descended with him were climbing off the platform and heading for their stations. He stared from one stubborn face to another, then raised his voice a full octave as he shrilled, "I'll have each and every one of you before the diplomat!"

"Good," one of the newcomers replied. "It's about time we got some answers."

"And stopped this nonsense of double watches and no clear orders," added another voice.

"We've overloaded the platform," someone else observed. "And there's still more coming this way."

A voice from the back cried, "Platform, mount!"

At the last moment before the rails slid up and the dais began its ascent, Wander grabbed hold of Digs' robe and pulled him off. Their move went unnoticed, as the platform's rise drew a chorus of shouts from those still streaming toward it. One monitor leaned over the rails and promised, "We'll send it right back for you!"

"Come down here!" The senior monitor was almost dancing with helpless rage. "You have watches to serve!"

"Serve it yourself," drifted back the reply.

In the tumult and confusion, Wander gripped Digs' shoulder and hissed, "Tell him we'll scout our own system."

Digs turned disbelieving eyes toward him. "Have you gone absolutely deranged?"

"Do it."

Reluctantly Digs slipped over to where the senior monitor was watching helplessly as the platform melded with the distant ceiling. "Ah, someone should be watching our own skies."

The senior monitor wheeled about, for a moment unable to focus on him. "Eh? What's that you said?"

"In case there really is something coming in," Digs said. "Just to be on the safe side."

The senior monitor peered at him, his ancient chest heaving. "What's your name, Monitor?"

"Digs, Senior Monitor. And we're just probationary watch standers."

"Not for long." He turned back to those waiting for the platform to return and shouted, "Here's what a true monitor is made of!"

"Give him time," said a grim voice. "He'll learn."

The senior monitor's shoulders sagged. Defeat transformed him into a tired old man. "Go," he said to Digs. "Serve your watch."

Digs waited until they had rounded the first mind-amp before declaring, "I hope you know what you're doing."

"It's a chance," Wander replied. "Only a chance."

"Right." The pinched-faced young man snorted as he raced to keep up with Wander. "A chance to get ourselves fried by some new mind-gun."

"My friends are ten days overdue," Wander said. "More."

Digs remained silent until they had arrived at the station, seated themselves, and began the power-up procedure. Then he glanced worriedly at Wander and asked, "Do you think maybe it's time to give up on all that?"

"I can't," Wander replied stonily.

"But this risk we're taking, what if we're—"

"If I stop hoping I stop living," Wander said. "Stay back here if you want. I'll go look."

"No, no." Digs sighed as he reached over and triggered the amp. "Guess I've got to hope with you."

There was the now-familiar surge outward, but instead of flinging himself headlong across space, Wander hovered, swung out and around the fiery planet, then stopped.

She was there.

Faint tendrils spun across his awareness, like wafts of some familiar perfume almost lost upon a rising wind. But it was Consuela. He knew it instantly. Her concerns, her fears, her struggle against a loss of hope, just like him. And her love.

Digs was there alongside. *I sense something.*

It's all right.

At least I think I did. It's gone now. It felt like, I don't know. A message? The awareness shifted and focused upon him. *Was it that girl?*

Consuela. Yes. There was no doubt. *She is nearby.*

I wonder . . . Digs floated free, his thoughts a jumble, then finished, *I wonder what it would be like to have someone care enough to search for me.*

Wonderful, Wander replied simply. *Will you cover for me?*

An instant's scanning, then, *We're alone out here right now. Make it fast.*

Immediately he sped outward, traversing the accustomed route to Avanti, and said, *Urgent, Urgent, Avanti Port, Tower Control, come in.*

A moment's delay, then, *Avanti Port, Watch Communicator here.*

There was something different, a crispness to the response, which made Wander hesitate before responding, *This is a friend—*

I know who this is. Go ahead, Allegro.

Again he was forced to pause. Allegro was the Avanti sister planet. Clearly the words were meant for someone else. A listener. *Request update on Spaceship Avenger.*

Avenger still detained at Imperial Command. No reason given. Arnol supposedly under suspicion of some crime, but nothing has been substantiated. The chancellor himself has lodged a complaint, as you have probably heard. As soon as the ship is freed, arrives in Yalla, and payment is passed on, your planet will receive its share for the investment made in its construction. How received?

Clear. But not possible. Consuela could not be there. She could not. Imperial Command was on the exact opposite side of the Hegemony. There was no way she could extend herself that far, much less compose and leave a heartfelt message.

Our chancellor has also notified Imperial Command that the invading dragoons will not be released until Avenger and all her crew arrive safely at their destination. How received?

Clear. That much was good. So long as the dragoons were in captivity, Citadel's defenses remained in a weakened state.

You had something urgent?

Wander reflected a moment, then replied, *Only that I am uncertain if my visitors are still expected to arrive.*

It was the watch communicator's turn to hesitate. *Repeat, please.*

Wander did so, then felt an urgent mental prodding from Digs. *Signing off.*

He powered back, slid the headset from his temples, and turned toward his friend. Digs looked frantic. "Someone's coming."

—SEVENTEEN—

Mahmut looked in astonishment from one to the other. "You want what?"

"It was just a question," Guns replied. "We were just wondering if your caravan might hold a copy of astrogation computations."

"We thought you might have had cause to travel off the standard course from time to time," Tucker added.

"But to travel anywhere away from Hegemony light-ways without a pilot on board is strictly forbidden," Mahmut pointed out.

"Right," Guns agreed, despondent. "Sorry we asked."

They were seated in the caravan's transport, which held a private owner's cabin, a smaller version of the caravan's own luxurious setting. Rick drew his silk cushion to the gathering's edge so that he could sit with his back against a heavy wall-tapestry. Even from this distance, however, he could feel Abdul's gaze upon him. The merchant's son sat beside his father, his dark gaze glowering across the circle, boring angrily into Rick.

"Still, it is a strange request," Mahmut contemplated aloud. "For our companions to ask if we might keep astrogation texts within our records."

"Companions," Abdul said bitterly. "They are nothing more than hired help."

Mahmut turned his gaze toward his son. The side of Abdul's head was still swathed in bandages from where he had fallen and hit the control console when the ship had been struck by the stun bolt. "Such words, such an attitude," Mahmut chided gently, "for those who saved both your life and mine."

"No one is out to usurp your position," Tucker offered gently to Abdul, "as master of the caravan's guards."

Abdul flushed darkly as the words struck home. "A fat chance you would have if you tried," he snarled.

Guns sighed his way to his feet. "Forgive the intrusion," he said to Mahmut, keeping his gaze off Abdul. "We won't bother you any further."

"One moment, please," Mahmut said, motioning for Guns to resume his place. He spent a long moment stroking his beard, then mused, "Even if we were to possess such information, we could not give you access to our ship's computers. The chieftains have sealed Yalla tight."

"For how long?" Guns demanded.

Mahmut showed him open palms. "They did not say. They never do. Nor did they give a reason. It seldom lasts for more than a few days. But during that time, we are forbidden to leave the planet's surface. And any contact with the mother ship must be made through their communication system."

Abdul stared at his father, aghast. "You cannot be considering their demand!"

"Their *request*," Mahmut corrected. "A request from *friends*."

"They are not friends," Abdul spat. "They are mercenaries. They hire out to whoever has the gold to pay them."

"And yet they are honorable men," Mahmut said, "who not only saved us, but did not take advantage when we were offering surrender, and all we had was theirs for the taking."

"But, Father—"

"Hold," Mahmut said, showing sternness for the first time. "Go and ask our hosts if we might use one of their larger computers to tap into our shipboard records. Tell them it is a highly confidential matter and must be done on sealed circuits."

Abdul sat as one frozen to stone. "You cannot be serious."

Aquiline features tightened in a flash of sudden anger. "Dare you to defy your father and master of the caravan?"

Abdul blanched. "No, Father."

"That is very good," Mahmut said, his voice taut with quiet intensity. "I am extremely glad to hear it. Now go and carry out your orders."

"I hear and obey," the son said numbly, and forced himself to his feet. He cast a final venomous glance toward Rick before slipping through the portal.

There was a moment's awkward silence before Mahmut sighed, "An only son, growing into a young man, granted his first true command on this very voyage."

"As guard captain," Tucker said sympathetically. "Only to see it taken away from him and the honor of battle go to someone else."

"It does not matter that rumors abounded, nor that one of our allies disappeared on this very route," Mahmut agreed, glancing at the door with dark sorrow. "He saw my decision to take on extra guards as an indication that I trusted your fighting abilities more than his own."

"And the fact that we were the ones who rescued the

caravan," Guns added gravely, "only rubbed salt into the wound."

Mahmut managed a small smile. "You have growing sons of your own?"

"No, but I remember how it felt to be young and handling my first command station," Guns replied. "It's hard enough, without having a father to please."

"Then you will understand why I must apologize for my son's behavior," Mahmut said. "And why I tell you that nothing of our earlier discussion has been passed on."

"Including the true strength of our pods," Tucker said anxiously.

"Indeed. Your hold remains sealed by your own men. Your secret is safe." He looked from one face to the next. "I trust that your request for astrogation guidance is not an idle one."

Guns glanced at Tucker, who said, "Tell him."

"We think we have found the planet called Citadel," Guns said, turning back to Mahmut. "The lass here followed four ships out on an uncharted course this very morning."

"Just when the chieftains placed this planet on quarantine." Dark eyes peered at Consuela with fierce intensity. "Is this indeed the planet from which the firestones come?"

"I don't know," Consuela replied honestly. "I was looking for my friend. Nothing else."

"But it would make sense," Tucker offered. "There's no other reason for them to take such a risk."

"They're headed to one of the planets in that system," Guns added. "And we need to go there ourselves. Will you help us?"

Mahmut gave his beard another stroke, then nodded once. "Right now."

–Eighteen–

"What's this I hear of mutiny?" the diplomat demanded.
Wander and Digs had tried to lose themselves at the back of the crowd, but to their alarm, the senior monitor had ordered them to the front row. There they stood, unable to escape the diplomat's furious glare.

They had been summoned with the other few who had chosen to stand watch, after the panic and the fears of an invasion. For the first time that Wander could recall, the cavern was left utterly empty, the listening stations unattended. Wander followed the others into the meeting hall, and though his legs were quaking, allowed himself to be led down front.

A querulous voice from the back spoke up. "We were tired—"

"*Silence!*" At the front of the chamber, the diplomat's midnight robes swirled as he strode angrily up and down the dais. "It is unthinkable that what I have heard might be true. Especially when the emperor's own supreme pilot, the head of your sect, is at this very moment making way for Citadel."

A tight shudder passed through the assembly. Wander

glanced to his left, where Digs met his eye and gave a slight shrug of incomprehension. Wander looked to where the senior monitor stood on Digs' other side, and felt a chill of unreasoned fear when he realized that the unshakable old man was gray and sweating.

"Ah," the diplomat said with satisfaction, surveying the assembly. "I see that some of the elders among us recall the last time the emperor's pilot graced us with his presence. Good. Take note of what they have to tell you. Tomorrow you will all have the honor of explaining your behavior in person. And be forewarned that all who do not answer satisfactorily will be invited to try a second time." The smile that suddenly creased the diplomat's features was perilous. "With Imperial dragoons there to assist you."

Wander shared the assembly's second tremor, but for a different reason. The emperor's pilot and more Imperial soldiers arrived *tomorrow*.

The diplomat turned his attention to the few monitors who stood alongside Digs and Wander on the front row. "Despite the fact that we were facing a possible attack, you were the only ones to stand to your stations. I shall allow the Supreme Pilot to determine your rewards. Except for you," he said, his gaze focusing upon Wander and Digs. "Stand forth, the both of you."

Wander took the step forward on shaking legs and waited.

"Our two youngest watch standers have shamed you all," he said to the assembly, his eyes remaining upon Wander. "You are both hereby awarded full status. Welcome to the ranks, Monitors."

"Thank you, sir," Wander said, his own voice a dull echo of Digs' triumphant response.

"It is traditional for a new monitor to be granted a boon. Name your request."

Wander did not need to think it out. "We'd like to return to duty."

He could feel Digs turning a dumbfounded gaze his way and shot a swift elbow into his friend's ribs. Digs jerked back to full alert and said, "The stations are unmanned, and we still don't know what's out there."

A gaze cold as space observed them a moment longer, then the diplomat said quietly, "Your request is noted. Dismissed. The rest of you, stand at attention as your betters depart."

Eyes upon the floor at his feet, Wander followed Digs through the silent assembly. As they approached the hall's main portals, a voice to one side hissed, "We too have made note of your request."

"Traitors," another seethed.

When the portals were closed behind them, they walked the empty hallway in echoing stillness until Digs said, "I hope your friends show up. Otherwise we may not have long to enjoy our new status."

Wander nodded and quickened his pace. "We have to hurry."

–Nineteen–

They came in the late afternoon, a full contingent of guards gathered about Abdul, who stepped forward and said, "We are ready."

"Is that so." Tucker rose to his feet from the gaming table. "You hear that, Guns? They're ready."

"Ready for what?"

"A very good question, that is. Ready for what, I ask as well, bringing along a full bevy of armed soldiers."

"You wanted to communicate with the mother ship," Abdul retorted. "It is a rare privilege to be permitted into the tribe's quarters. This is your honor guard."

"A privilege," Tucker repeated, his eyes casting doubt on all they touched. "Well, Guns, it looks like your predictions have come true after all."

"Aye," the grizzled veteran agreed, and demanded of Abdul, "Where's Mahmut?"

Flanked by the guards, it was possible to see how the desert blood flowed in Abdul's veins, in the aquiline features, the knife-edge to his chin and cheekbones, the glittering cast to his eyes. "Alas, my honorable father has been called to a meeting of the chieftains."

"How timely," Guns muttered, and motioned to Rick. "You completed that work I set for you?"

"Not yet," Rick said, his eyes still on Abdul.

"Then you'll just have to stay put and do your work."

"But, Guns—"

"That's an order, flyer!"

"Aye, aye, Guns." Rick turned and stomped off to the stone-draped pod.

Abdul watched the exchange in consternation. "But he is to come with us!"

"Why?" Tucker demanded, shifting his bulk up oppressively close. "A pod flyer's not required to draw information from your memory banks."

Guns stepped up alongside. "Just what is it you've got in store?"

"Nothing, he, I . . . nothing." Angrily Abdul gathered himself. "If you are coming, come now!"

"Right with you." Guns nodded to Tucker, turned back to the pod. "First I need to make sure the boy understands his business."

"No weapons. You will be searched," Abdul added.

"Of course we will." Guns disappeared as Tucker raised his arms and submitted to a rough jostling by the guards.

When Guns returned from speaking with Rick, he walked over to Consuela and said softly, "You mind coming with us, lass?"

"But you don't need me."

"Ah, but we do." He handed her the cloak he carried. "Might do best if you cover yourself a bit more."

"But I—"

"Humor an old man," he said, keeping his back to the suspicious guards. "Here, let me help you." He slung it over her shoulders, then fastened it at her neck with a glittering silver clasp. "There. Much better."

The robe's clasp was heavy, with a single blue stone at its center. She fingered it and asked softly, "What is this all about, Guns?"

"Nothing, I hope." He turned around and allowed himself to be thoroughly searched.

Abdul pointed at Consuela and demanded, "She comes with us."

"Wouldn't have it any other way," Guns agreed cheerfully. But when the guards moved toward Consuela, both he and Tucker stepped in close. They hovered over the guards as they searched her, and observed in menacing silence. The guards hastily completed their frisking and stepped back.

"This way," Abdul said, smiling fiercely.

"Hang on a second," Tucker said. He ducked inside the transport and came out with a small flat rectangle. He handed it over for inspection, saying, "Wouldn't help us to go unless we had a portable memory for storing the information."

Abdul accepted the box, flipped open the lid, keyed the console, nodded, and handed it to one of the guards.

"Just your basic portable set," Guns offered.

Clearly the guard agreed. His fingers searched out the catches, opened the back slot, checked everything carefully, then handed it back. Abdul rapped out, "We go."

The tunnel was large enough for the three visitors to be flanked on all sides. The few tribesfolk they passed refused even to look their way.

A hundred paces farther in, the tunnel opened into yet another cavern. They were led toward a series of small transport-platforms and instructed to step aboard. Instantly the railings slid up, the platforms lifted, and they were away.

Consuela did not try to hide her interest as they traversed tunnel after tunnel. This was not some impover-ished series of underground dwellings, but a civilization rich in culture and tradition. Even at their high speed, she could make out how all the internal tunnels were decorated with brilliant murals of vibrant scenes. The caverns them-selves were equally impressive. Far overhead, translucent skylights allowed in soft filtered light. They illuminated walled worlds of green, for each of the caverns was cen-tered upon an underground spring. Water bubbled into lakes and carefully managed rivulets. Trees bloomed in gar-dens of flowers and vegetables and fruit vineyards. Birds with brilliant coloration flitted alongside their platforms, singing strident challenges to these other flyers.

They entered yet another tunnel, which took an upward slant. Higher and higher they climbed, leaving Consuela to wonder how they could make such an ascent and yet still remain underground.

Eventually the platforms landed in an antechamber whose vaulted ceiling rose to a high peak. Abdul alighted and brusquely motioned them forward. "In here."

They followed him through a pair of powered doors, which slid open at their approach. Consuela took a step in-side and stopped with a gasp.

The room was ringed with communication and com-puting equipment. Above it rose great windows, which looked out over a billowing yellow sea.

They had climbed up inside the center of a mountain, she realized, stepping closer to the thick sheets of glass. They were now so high that the planet's perpetual storms were below them. The clouds of sand rose and puffed like ghostly yellow waves, churning and swirling in glistening streams.

"Of course," Tucker said. "Transmission would be better if they could stay above the worst of the gales."

"Enough," Abdul snapped. "Give me the memory console."

"Just a minute there," Tucker responded, and turned to Guns. "You know this rig?"

"Trained on one just like it," Guns affirmed.

Tucker turned back to Abdul and said, "The deal was, you connect us with the ship's onboard memory, then we are left alone."

"But I—"

"Alone," Tucker repeated. "Your father agreed to this."

Abdul looked from one to the other in helpless fury, then spun about and began coding in. He waited a second, then snarled, "Be quick about it," and stomped for the doors, signaling the guards to follow.

Guns stepped to the console, searched a moment, grunted when he recognized the configuration, and swiftly made the connections from the communicator to his portable set.

"Seal the circuits," Tucker reminded him.

"Just seeing to that," Guns agreed, pulling up a chair and working swiftly. "Okay, that's done."

Immediately Tucker moved up close to Consuela and said, "We're in. Stand at the ready."

Consuela took a confused step backward and asked, "Ready for what?"

"Ready for the coding," Guns replied.

Consuela looked from one to the other. "But I don't—"

"Here is the coding from Mahmut." Tucker drew a paper from his pocket, unfolded it, and began droning out a series of numbers and letters, giving time for Guns to punch them in. There followed a tense moment, until Guns announced, "Receiving."

"Make it fast," Tucker said.

Another span of a dozen heartbeats, then, "All done."

"Check for error," Tucker urged. "We won't get a second chance."

Another hesitation, then, "Up and running."

"Here it comes then," Tucker muttered, and stepped toward the portal.

Instantly the doors slid back to reveal Abdul and the guards. The merchant's son was smiling yet again, an evil grimace that stretched his entire face out of shape. The guards stood with blasters at the ready. "You are finished," Abdul announced.

"We were just about to tell you the same thing," Guns agreed easily.

"My father's orders have been carried out," Abdul announced. "You have received the secret information. But you will never have an opportunity to use it."

"What about the lass here? She's done nothing wrong." Tucker drew her close with a heavy arm on her shoulders, then said, "Alarm, alarm."

"What was that?" Abdul snapped.

"He said, alarm," Guns agreed. "And that's exactly what we think. It's *alarming* that you would think of dishonoring your father like this."

"I have done exactly as he ordered," Abdul retorted, his face flaming. "It is you who poisoned his mind with thoughts of honor, when you will take your coin and turn against him."

"The only one who's turned against him is you," Tucker said, risking a nervous glance around and out of the windows. He turned back, gave Guns a slight shrug.

"I am protecting our caravan!" Abdul rapped out. He signaled the guards forward.

Guns turned fully about, muttering, "What's going on here?"

"Maybe the storm stopped the signal," Tucker murmured and turned around as well, drawing Consuela with him as the guards moved to surround them.

"Yes, look well," Abdul said. "For you will never again see the light of day."

"Trouble," Guns muttered.

"The storm," Tucker agreed. "Should have thought of that."

"Too late for regrets," Abdul crowed. "You are now my . . ."

His words trailed off when one by one the guards murmured and pointed and cried out as a stone dot puffed up through the billowing sandstorm and shot toward them. Just outside the window, the guard pod stopped and hovered.

Tucker turned and announced, "Looks like the tables have turned."

"He won't shoot," Abdul cried, struggling to rally the nervous guards. "He wouldn't dare. He'd only be shooting his own men!"

"The lad," Guns replied, with his battle hardened grin, "doesn't have to shoot."

With an explosion so powerful that the windows quaked and the floor beneath their feet shivered, the pod erupted. The guards cowered and covered their heads, then slowly rose back when the windows held. They stared dumbfounded at a midnight black flyer shaped like the head of a spear.

"Lay down your weapons," Tucker ordered. "All of you."

"Shoot them!" Abdul screamed.

Guns leaned towards Consuela and rapped out, "Blade! Attack sequence *now!*"

Instantly a tongue of brilliant white energy shot from the front of the pod. Deftly the flyer maneuvered forward and sliced through window and wall as though they were butter.

That proved more than the guards had bargained for. They made for the portal in a mad rush. When Abdul tried to stop them, he was flung to the floor. Which meant he was the only outsider to witness the arrival of five other Blades from the depths of that deep blue sky.

Tucker swung around and said to Consuela, "Blade Three, go back and escort the transporter down."

Instantly one of the fighter-pods swung away and descended back into the billowing storm.

"Her brooch is a microphone," Abdul rasped, struggling to rise. "You tricked me."

"Stay where you are," Tucker commanded, hefting one of the discarded blasters.

"Don't hurt him," Consuela pleaded.

"I ought to fry him to a crisp," Tucker grated. "But it would be a dishonor to his father, who is a man among men."

When Abdul realized he was not to be harmed, he turned his attention back to the melted windows and the pods beyond. His eyes narrowed. "Elemental trinium," he said. "I wonder what the emperor would pay to learn that rebel mercenaries were operating attack pods of elemental trinium."

"I wonder how well you'd serve your father without a tongue," Tucker replied.

"Hold," Guns ordered, then said to Abdul, "You should be glad, matey. They're the only thing that kept you from sitting in the belly of a stinking slaver."

"Gratitude is one of the many traits his father failed to teach him," Tucker said, glowering.

Guns motioned toward the window and announced, "Our transport is here."

The first Blade to have arrived, the one piloted by Rick, switched off his brilliant power-lance. Gently Rick then nudged the outer wall, pressing in, shoving through rock and molten glass, sending dust and stones billowing inward. The communication equipment sparked and fizzled as it was pushed farther and farther back. The Blade shifted to one side, making a larger space where the transporter could move in and land alongside.

When the Blade's portal opened, Guns stepped forward and said, "You took your time about it, lad."

"I could scarcely make out a word," Rick responded. "It sounded like you were talking inside a machine shop. I finally decided it was better to be safe than sorry."

"You did right," Tucker said, motioning Consuela forward and into the transport. "Another minute and we might have been gone for good."

Rick stood in the wreckage of the communications tower, ignoring Abdul entirely. "Where do we go now?"

"Out and away," Guns said, the memory console tucked under one arm. "There's work to do, and not a second to lose." He patted Rick's shoulder. "You did well, lad. I'm proud of you."

—TWENTY—

"You have to sleep."

Wander pushed the hand away. "Power me up."

"It's not going to help your friends any if they arrive and find you flat on your back, your brain melted down."

"I'm all right, I tell you." Yet despite his best efforts, Wander could not fully erase the slur from his voice. His words seemed to slide out, melding together into a toneless tangle. "Hook me back up."

Digs looked pained. "You've been on three watches and more without a break."

"I have to," Wander replied stubbornly.

"You *can't*." Digs ripped the headset from Wander's hands. "Look, just pull your cushions off the chair and lie there on the floor. I'll stay hooked up the whole time."

Wander tried to argue, but he didn't have the strength. "I don't know what to tell you to look for."

Digs gave a humorless smile. "Sounds just like the orders I've been following for weeks."

Wander found it necessary to use both hands to push himself erect. When he bent over to lay out the cushions, he almost fell over. "It's less than six hours before the Hegemony vessel is due," he said, stretching out with a groan.

"I can read a chrono as good as you."

Wander suddenly found he could not keep his eyes open. "What happens if my friends don't get here before the Imperial ship and its dragoons?"

Digs was silent a long moment, his face growing steadily grimmer. Finally he said quietly, "I don't know."

But Wander was already asleep.

Tucker said to Consuela, "There's no doubt?"

"None." This close, Consuela did not even need to power up. The air seemed to buzz with static power. She pointed through the viewport and said, "The next planet after this one is where Wander is being held."

"All right, lads." Guns kept his voice to a low murmur, as though talking quietly would keep them from being detected. "Unhook the Blades."

Tucker gave a satisfied nod to the transport's first officer. "Well done."

"It wasn't me," the young man protested, and pointed to where Guns sat in the navigator's seat. "All I did was follow his instructions."

"Aye, well, congratulations to the both of you." Tucker stared out the front visor at the pitted surface of the system's fifth planet. Even at this close proximity, the sun was so swollen it blazed about the planet's edges, surrounding the globe with a fiery halo. "Wonder what possessed them to put a garrison in a red giant's system."

"I seem to recall the pilot Dunlevy saying something about this once having been the Hegemony's borders," Guns offered, unstrapping and standing up, massaging his back.

"Aye, well, I've served some miserable posts in my time,

but this is one place I'm glad to have missed."

"You and me both." Guns patted the first officer's shoulder and said, "You'd best go ahead and plot our return course."

"Me?" The young officer showed genuine alarm.

"You saw what I did. The computer does most of the work. Make preparations for a swift departure for Avanti. We may be in a hurry when we return."

"Aye, aye, Guns."

There was a rough scraping through the transport's roof, and a pair of shadows flitted in front of the viewport. For the voyage across uncharted space, the Blades had melded their shields together and bonded tightly about the transport. A voice declared over the intercom, "All Blades but yours are freed, Guns."

"Prepare for action, but don't power up your weapons," Guns replied. "We don't know what those boyos on Citadel can and cannot detect." He turned to Tucker and said, "I better be off, then."

Tucker offered him a meaty paw. "Good hunting, matey."

Guns met him with an iron-hard grip. "Aye, we'll give them a run for their money."

"More than that," Tucker said. "We'll be watching for your signal."

Guns nodded in Consuela's direction and said, "And I for yours."

When Guns had slipped through the portal and entered his Blade, Tucker said to her, "Time to hook up."

She hid her grimace, as all the troopers were watching her every move. Consuela slid behind the console, fitted on the headset, and powered up. Instantly the distant buzz rose to an angry swirl of power. But no voices. There was no communication, just an incredibly focused source of listening.

Thankfully, none of the focus was directed at her. In fact, everything seemed to be reaching so far out beyond the system's borders that anything this close went undetected. Gingerly she inched up the power dial, reaching out, ever fearful of being discovered.

When the signal rapped through her headset, it shocked her so that she leapt to her feet, jamming the seat back and over the edge. She kept one hand pressed to the headset upon her temple as she leaned over and powered back. She stayed like that an instant longer, observing, focusing more tightly about the source of the voices, and feeling all the blood drain from her face. Finally she powered off completely, raised up to face Tucker, and said quietly, "We have trouble."

— TWENTY-ONE —

Wander awoke to the smell of hot soup and a nudge from Digs. He opened his eyes, rubbed away the grit that matted his lashes, and saw his friend offering him a steaming mug and a sandwich. He struggled upright and said, "I feel as though I just shut my eyes."

Digs showed grim humor. "You've been snoring away for almost three hours."

"So long?" Wander rubbed a crick from his neck. "How did you get those? I thought you said you'd keep watch."

"I was only gone a minute." The grim lines deepened. "Besides, you'll be needing all your strength and wits."

Wander took a sip and felt the warmth course through him. "What's the matter?"

"The Hegemony ship has arrived early," Digs said, and a flicker of fear rose within his gaze.

———

"Await my signal," Wander said, fitting his headset into place.

Digs looked at him uncertainly. "You're sure you want to do this?"

"Unless you have a better idea." Wander settled back, took a deep breath, then another.

"I've never heard of anyone trying anything like this." Digs' hand hovered over the controls. "Probably because they knew they'd end up getting fried."

"My friends are risking their lives to come for us. At least I hope they are." Wander regarded his friend. "How can I do any less?"

Digs nodded acceptance and fitted his own headset into place. "Just be careful."

"Is your damping on full?"

"Don't worry about me," Digs replied, nerves turning his tone sharp. "Just go out, do it, and get back."

Wander closed his eyes. Took another breath. "Ready."

"Here goes, then."

There was too much risk of him getting out and not being able to make it back. He needed a back-up, someone to remain at the borders of his activity, watching carefully, ready to draw him home. That was Digs' task, to protect himself with a fully damped headset, observing both what Wander did and how he was, with one hand ever ready on the controls.

Even so, Wander was a mere hair's breadth away from sheer terror.

Digs did exactly as they planned, powering up just a fraction, enough for Wander to raise his awareness above Citadel's scarred surface, hover, and collect himself.

Then Digs rammed the power controls to full.

The force was enough to have sent Wander's awareness rocketing to the Hegemony's farthest borders and beyond. But he resisted, remaining exactly where he was, though the force threatened to split his mind into a billion shimmering fragments.

Finally he moved, harboring the force, riding it like a

whirlwind, drifting up to the Imperial ship, seeking out the communication link. A silver thread of mind-amp power flickered outward, the Supreme Pilot and his two assistant pilots communicating with Imperial Command. Without making contact, Wander's harnessed force was sufficient for him to make the instant identification.

The pilot noticed something at the periphery of his extended awareness and began the turning. It was what Wander had wanted, a crack in their concentration. Immediately he pounced.

Releasing all the force that he had been holding back, Wander gave it a face of utter frenzy. He *screamed* out, using his focused power as a flashing mental fist, attacking down, forcing his way into the pilots' protected chamber, shrilling with all his might, *DANGER HERE. DANGER. CITADEL UNDER ATTACK. WITHDRAW. DANGER. WITHDRAW IMMEDIATELY. SAVE YOURSELVES.*

He stayed only long enough to see all three pilots retreat in gibbering horror, their minds stunned to insensibility by the suddenness and the force of his attack.

Then he moved away.

The power still coursing through him, unleashed and unchecked, he circled back and around the planet, stopping at each outward-focused lance of attention. One by one he attacked them with a diving force, a biting strike of unexpected fury, the words always the same. *DANGER. DANGER. ALARM. ALARM.*

The monitors' mind-amps granted him an unexpected advantage. They opened and focused the monitors' attention, which meant that his attack was met not with defense, but rather by focused and amplified openness. Instantly he realized that here was the reason for the Citadel's secrecy: *A monitor had no defenses other than concealment.*

One moment, the monitors searched the far reaches in

utter certainty that they were concealed and thus invincible. The next, an apparition flooded directly into their minds, screaming alarm. By the time Wander had made one swift circle of Citadel, there was not a single focused monitor-beam remaining upon the planet.

Wander did not hesitate. Instantly he sent the signal to Digs and heaved a mental sigh of relief as the power eased back. He continued outward, but not far, extending only through the system, searching with open liberty and shouting in frantic haste another word now, over and over, calling out her name. *Consuela!*

One moment he was alone and lacerated by the fear that all was still in vain. The next, he was enveloped by a mind and heart as eager and yearning as his own.

They spun together for a half-dozen heartbeats, locked in the embrace of those who no longer have room nor time for barriers. Their love was as boundless as space, their joy as brilliant as the red orb shining overhead.

Gradually, reluctantly, Wander eased himself away. *I must hurry.*

Wander. Oh, Wander.

Listen to me, beloved. We must go, and now. He offered her a mental shake, in the form of a shimmering diamond that flashed toward her and exploded with a spark of unexpected power. She jerked away, relinquishing her hold. He asked, *Where is the ship Avenger?*

Gone, I mean, we are just the transport and the Blades. Consuela struggled to collect herself. There was an instant's pause, then, *I told the others you are here.*

Where . . . oh, I see now. He located the ships as they rounded the fifth planet and headed toward Citadel. The six Blades and the battered transport seemed so puny, set against the might of the empire. But there was no choice. He braced himself and said again, *We must hurry.*

We are ready. And she was. Quivering with taut eagerness. *Tell us what to do*.

Swiftly he sketched out his plan, stopping at intervals for her to repeat it to the others. When he was finished, there was a brief pause, then Consuela said, *They agree*.

It startled him, this military-like acceptance. No argument, no doubt, no hesitation. For the first time since the kidnapping, Wander felt himself thrilled by the sudden flood of unbridled hope. *I must go and prepare*.

Swiftly they embraced, a gift of closing together, moving beyond the realm of words, giving and receiving the rapture of love granted a future.

—Twenty-two—

As the mind-amp's power receded, Wander felt his own physical strength drain away. He turned toward Digs without raising his head from the chair. "You'd better be going."

"Are you all right?"

"Fine," he said weakly, willing strength back into his limbs. He could be feeble later. "Hurry."

The concern in Digs' gaze was suddenly replaced by a blaze of hope. "You found them?"

"They're coming." Wander waved him away. "Hurry."

Digs leaped from the chair. "This should be easy."

"Why do you say that?"

His friend gave a genuine grin for the first time in days. "Can't you hear?"

Wander stilled his breath and listened as wails rose from the distance. "It worked," he said, vastly relieved.

Digs raced for the mind-amp's entry, then hesitated. "You won't forget me?"

"We are leaving this place together," Wander promised firmly, his energy returning. *"Hurry."*

Digs gave him a grin so wide it almost split his face. "Watch me fly," he said, and was gone. He raced down the aisle between the mind-amps, screaming at the top of his voice, "Alarm! Alarm! The amps are blowing! Out of the cavern, everybody! Hurry!"

The call was swiftly picked up by others, and Wander heard the sound of racing feet and frantic voices scrambling by outside his amp.

Grimly he switched to Digs' seat, fitted on the headset, and reached for the controls. He had time for one brief hope that it would not be necessary to power up fully another time, especially not alone, especially when he was already so weak. Then he switched the amp back on and focused outward.

To his vast relief, the Imperial ship was retreating.

The great dark vessel was moving up and away from Citadel. It could not attain n-space transport, not without the pilots for guidance. But it could and did place greater distance between itself and what it thought was the source of attack. An attack unheard of in the Hegemony annals. An attack not made with standard weapons, but rather launched directly upon the piloting network, locking the ship down, holding it trapped within an alien system, without even lightways to guide it away. The captain was no doubt fighting panic among his crew.

Even so, Wander could sense the risk of pods being launched, Imperial dragoons pouring out, hunting the unseen assailant. He switched his attention and saw the seven tiny ships flitting toward him.

He turned and reached out. *Consuela?*

Here. The response was immediate. Terse with eagerness.

Your course is correct. Hurry.

Guns sees the Imperial vessel. Are they attacking?

Not yet.

We are passing through the fire storm. No, I see, it's your

atmosphere. A pause, then a subdued, *What a horrible place.*
    Yes.

    Strike in thirty seconds. Wait, wait. Rick sees the canyon!
And the fortress. Yes! There it is! Oh, Wander, we are coming!

    Wander felt a hand on his shoulder and knew it was
time. *We are leaving now.*

    We?

    Oh. I forgot. He felt Digs shake his shoulder again. *There*
are two of us.

—TWENTY-THREE—

"Attack mode!" Rick powered his weapons systems to full and steadied his course to skim just above the canyon's scarred and pitted floor. Overhead swept a perpetual storm covering, not of clouds, but of fire. "By me, Blades!"

"Blade Four, in formation."

"Blade Six, roger that."

"First Officer here. We are adhering to your track. Remember we need a hole large enough for the transport."

"Target in sight," Rick announced, his voice a knife edge. He popped the guards off his foregun triggers, sighted, and shouted, "Firing one!"

The bolt seemed to drift down, impossibly slow for an energy missile, giving notice to the gallons of adrenaline that pumped his heart rate to overdrive. Then the missile struck, followed swiftly by a second, and, "We have an opening! Prepare the troops!"

"Roger that." It was Tucker. "Guns, any sign of the dragoons?"

"All clear. Just don't hang around."

"Not an instant more than necessary."

Rick tucked his shoulders in tight, as though trying to

draw the Blade in narrower. At his speed, the hole seemed impossibly small. But he entered with room to spare, as did the transport. Then he stopped. He had to.

"Incredible!" came Tucker's hoarse exclamation. "What are they?"

"Power-amps," Rick said. "They have to be."

Stretching out as far as they could see was a cavern of impossible size. Their energy bolts had both sucked out all the air and filled the space with dust. Through this maelstrom they could see the dark flickering rings below, and the veins of light planted in both floor and ceiling.

It was Tucker who broke the frozen tableau. "On to the center, Blades. Move."

They dropped to the cavern floor, hunted, found the first platform near their entry-point, kept moving, and finally Rick shouted, "Central platform dead ahead!"

"Guard our flanks, Blades," Tucker said, and then went on, "Set her down easy."

"Like a baby," the transport's flight officer agreed.

The transport drifted over and down, settling at the platform's center. Over the internal communications system and all-channel radio as well, Tucker shouted, "Platform, mount!"

Instantly the rails rose up, and the platform began its gentle descent.

–TWENTY-FOUR–

The explosion rocked the floor of Wander's compartment. Digs showed no fear whatsoever. Instead, he raised his fists to the ceiling, his robe falling back to expose the dragon tattoo swirling down his right arm. His neck so taut the muscles stood out like cords, he shouted, *"Yes!"*

"I hate this waiting," Wander said. Somehow the tension left him quieter, more focused, counting the seconds like endless days.

"Your plan is a good one. You're sure they know which chamber?"

"I gave them the clearest instructions I could."

"Then they'll be here any moment."

But they weren't. Instead, there was only silence. Alarms sounded in the distance, then halted, then started back. Nothing else. The waiting stretched out so long Wander felt his nerves were snapping, one by one, threads as taut as the chamber's atmosphere, splitting under the unending strain, leaving him tottering on the brink of—

Through the heavy portal there came the sudden chinking of metal on stone. Wander leapt up and shouted in a voice not his own, "Open!"

Chief Petty Officer Tucker stormed in, eyes blazing, weapon at the ready. "Time to fly, lad."

Another trooper fitted through the portal, spotted Digs, and raised his weapon. "Wait!" Wander shouted. "He's a friend!"

Tucker eyed the stranger and demanded, "He's coming?"

"Yes," Wander and Digs said together.

"Let's be off, then."

Together they raced down the corridor, around one bend after another, until the transport came into view.

The portal opened, spilling out a brown-haired figure in a gray spacesuit who came racing over, her arms outstretched and hair streaming, eyes wide and filled to overflowing. She flew into Wander's embrace, holding him with a force that promised never to let him go, saying things to his ear that he could not hear for the pounding of his own heart, a heart that shimmered with the fullness of hope and promise.

Tucker let the reunion continue for a brief moment, then said gruffly, "Into the transport. Hurry, now. We're not out of this yet."

The transport lifted and started before the last trooper was settled, heading back to the platform chamber. The chamber's door lay shattered upon the corridor floor. They entered the chamber, hovered above the floor, and Tucker said, "Everybody fixed down tight? Take a good grip." He then said into the microphone, "All right, Rick. Easy does it."

For a moment there was nothing, then the floor below them began to glow. Stronger and stronger, until there was a rending tremor, which rose until the very air seemed to shake.

Then the Blade's energy lance came into view, prodding

a hole that grew and grew, and with it came a shrieking wind, powering through the chamber's destroyed portal, pouring air from all the corridors, a hurricane of air and dust and moisture. It streamed through the hole where the Blade had been, pulling the transport down through the ceiling and into the mind-amp chamber.

"You're sure about what you told us," Tucker demanded, "all the monitors' private chambers have airtight doors?"

"It's a fact known by all," Digs confirmed. "When I first arrived, they still held regular safety drills, everyone going into the nearest chamber and sealing it down. But then the new diplomat arrived, and all that was stopped. The alarms sounded when you attacked. Even the ones who never practiced the drill will know to go into their chambers. There is emergency food and water in each. They will be safe."

A voice over the intercom said, "Shall I blast these amps?"

"No," Wander ordered. "It could crack the planet in half."

Tucker looked doubtful. "It would save us all a lot of worry in the future, lad."

"It's not necessary," Wander assured him, both his hands captured by Consuela's. "I've found a way to protect us."

"Eh? How's that?"

Wander shared a look of love and joy with Consuela, and replied, "I've learned the secret behind Citadel's mystery."

Epilogue

Rick stopped in front of the carnival entrance and said, "I sure hope I know what I'm doing."

It was here that their adventure had begun. An unexpected shift to new challenges came through the same roller coaster which glittered and soared just up ahead. Consuela looked up at him, her eyes shining. "You have prayed about this, haven't you?"

"All last night and most of today," Rick confirmed.

"And have you been given a sense of direction?"

"So clear and so strong," Rick hesitated, then finished, "I feel as though God has been waiting for me to ask the right question."

Daniel moved up to stand alongside Consuela. He said for them both, "Then you should do as you feel called."

"I will," Rick agreed. He looked upward at the stars, their light white and beckoning against the dark sky. "I just wish I could be sure I'm doing the right thing."

"God's promise of blessing must at times be enough." Bliss took her husband's hand and smiled up at Rick. "He urges us to set out upon His chosen road, accepting that there will be times when only He is able to see the way ahead."

Consuela looked from one face to the next, the three friends standing there around her, feeling sad and excited and happy and confused all at once. The carnival's jangling noise seemed held at bay by the same calm that reached through the unsettled storm and granted peace to her heart. And that defined her own path.

As though reading her thoughts, Daniel echoed his wife's words. "God promises change. Just as He said to Abraham, He tells us, I will bless you. And in doing so, He opens up a future. A future of hope, of change, of renewal. Like Abraham, though, you may be called to a land whose name you don't even know. And if that happens, your trust must grow to meet the challenge."

Consuela shivered, half in anticipation, half in fear, and clutched her bundle tighter.

"You must realize," Daniel went on, "that in fully accepting the Lord as your God, you accept the future He has chosen for you."

"That is how I feel," Rick said solemnly.

"Me too," Consuela agreed.

Daniel turned solemn eyes to Consuela. "Then go. We will miss you. But our prayers will be with you always."

Bliss offered her as much of a smile as the sadness in her eyes would permit. "It was so wonderful to see you and your mother together."

"And to see her so well," Consuela agreed. The words brought another bloom of sadness and longing, and for a moment she faltered.

As though reading Consuela's mind, Bliss patted her arm and assured her, "Your mother has blessed your decision. She is well, and she is praying for you. That is a gift and a sign both, or at least it seems that way to me."

"Thank you." Consuela hugged them close, first Bliss and then Daniel and then Rick, trying to seal their presence into her heart for all time.

Together they turned and entered the carnival. The crowds and music and noise and lights flitted about them, leaving them untouched. The stillness and peace moved with them, granting the action and the moment a sense of rightness beyond thought, beyond words.

They stopped before the roller coaster. As Rick moved over to buy the four tickets, Daniel hugged her a second time and said, "We will pray for you."

"Each and every day," Bliss agreed, her voice suddenly unsteady.

Rick returned, and together they mounted the platform, handing the man four tickets so they all could go forward. But it was only Consuela who seated herself. Rick held her parcel until she was settled, then handed it to her before moving back to join Daniel and Bliss. He called over, "Do you think I can ever go back to that other world?"

"If it is God's will," Consuela replied, as sure of that as she was of anything in her entire life.

The roller coaster started forward with a jerk. Consuela pulled the Bible from her parcel and wrapped her arms tightly around it, pressing it to her chest. As the roller coaster gained speed, she turned back and called out a single word to the three people who stood and waved her onward.

"Friends!"